Igbe

A dance with the spirits

JAEL MUDIAGA

IGBE

A dance with the spirits

JAEL MUDIAGA

This book is dedicated to my late mum, Mrs. Miriam Isoko. Your strong will stays with me forever.

PROLOGUE

April 1st 1970.

Kokori, Delta State, Nigeria.

The three women and their ten children were dragged roughly to the centre of the market square, where the villagers scattered about, shouted obscenities at them.

"Uuuuh…" The women booed at them, tapping their fingers repeatedly, against their mouths.

"Eshu! Witches!" said one woman, trying unsuccessfully to keep her wrapper tied under her armpit from loosing. "You have killed your husband, our Chief, so you can consume all of his wealth!" She cried in their native Urhobo tongue.

"I am innocent!" cried the youngest woman forced to sit on the ground. "It's these monsters that call themselves senior wives! They were jealous of my dear Chief's love for me. So, they conspired to kill him, to leave my children fatherless." She dragged her little boy and girl against her bosom and wailed. "They have made me a widow at an early age, hah!"

"May thunder strike your foul mouth!"

Snapped the eldest wife. "You dare to call me a murderer? Where is my respect?"

The second wife hissed long and loud as she looked menacingly at the youngest wife. "He who is guilty is the one who has much to say. It is you and your children that are witches. Husband snatcher!"

"Silence, women!" An elderly man broke from the crowd to stand in front of them. "Enough of your bickering." He snarled. "Today, the priestess will decide. Give way!" He shouted to the crowd and immediately there was silence as the faint sound of a drum could be heard from a distance. The thirteen people on the ground wore a look of horror on their faces and the children shuddered.

The crowd broke out in an excited frenzy as the Igbe dancers came into view, clearing the way for them, as they danced to the centre of the square.
The four female dancers dressed in white wrappers only, waving their white hand fans and beating it against their lap, parted in half to give way to another group. These group of women were more matured and were heavily made up. They formed a circle and stomped their feet in rhythmically and in unison to the drums beaten by the seven hefty and shirtless men, wearing only white knickers.

One of the women carried a 5 feet 3 inches mirror. Another a life cock, and another a basin, balanced properly with a cloth on her head. The fourth carried white native chalk in her outstretched left palm. They were all looking straight ahead as if they were headed to no place in particular. They stopped in front of the family seated on the ground and as they separated, the clouds gathered suddenly, lightning struck and thunder rumbled, causing the crowd to shift uneasily backwards. Their circle broke to reveal the priestess who was covered with a white scarf.

She took it off dramatically and the people gave an excited gasp. The priestess was a very large lady in her forties. She had more chalk drawings on her face than any of the others, she was also clothed in a white wrapper but had red bands on each wrist and ankle. She stood like a warrior in front of the suspects, then suddenly danced round to face the crowd, with her legs wide apart. The drumbeats did not stop but were now softer.

"Emo Kokori, wadoh!" She shrieked in Urhobo language, punching her right fist straight into the air.

"Eeeh!" They all replied in unison, punching their fists too.

"Emo Agege, wadoh!"

"Eeeh!"

She narrowed her eyes at the suspects as she swivelled. "On a straight line." They formed a vertical line in front of her, from her right to left, from senior to junior. Apparently, they all knew how it was done, except for the two little kids, who had to be assisted by their older stepbrother.

The priestess collected the chalk from the woman holding it out. She broke the chalk, offered half for all thirteen of them to eat. Then she used the other half to draw a straight line in front of them. The little girl who's not more than two started to cry at the taste of chalk on her tongue.

"Silence!" The priestess snapped. Shocked, the baby slammed her tiny fist over her mouth to keep from crying out.
She then returned the chalk and the woman with the mirror stepped forward to the first wife, holding the mirror out.

"Look at Agege." The priestess commanded her. She looked, gasped and turned away. The fourth child, a boy of thirteen years old waited impatiently for his turn, craning his neck to catch a glimpse of what they saw in the mirror. He braced himself, as his turn finally came. He frowned at his reflection, looked at the priestess as if to say 'is that it? No big scary monster?' He was disappointed. His sister of fifteen years had better plans, as soon as the mirror stood in front of her, she grinned charmingly at herself and raised her hip slightly, after all, it was not every day you got to see a real-life mirror. This was so much better than looking at your reflection in the stream. She noticed the lady holding the mirror, sneering at her, so she quickly looked down.

The priestess cleared her throat as the mirror lady backed off. "You have seen Agege, the god of the Igbes. Do anyone of you have a confession to make before she strikes you with madness?"

The wives shuffled uneasily, while the crowd mumbled. "Fine. Wash your hands in that basin. For it contains water from Agege's great river. This act signifies that your hands are clean and you have nothing to do with the death of Chief Onawata Okpako's death. Wash!"
The wives matched almost defiantly to wash their hands in the basin placed in front of them. Their children followed suit.

"You" she pointed at the first wife "Cross the line, kneel before me and swear –that if you killed your husband, may Agege make you mad by the spilling of the blood of the cock."

"I, Erekakwe, swear by Agege" she lifted her right palm and looked up as she spoke boldly. "If I killed my husband, Chief Onawata, may I run mad by the spilling of the blood of the cock!"

The priestess grabbed the cock and circled it over Erekakwe's head three times. The cock crowed loudly, no doubt, begging for its life. She repeated this action on the others, but for the little children, she just rolled the cock over their heads without asking them to swear. Then she stood dramatically looking around smugly. The moment all of them had been waiting for had finally arrived. The drums picked up-tempo.

"Agege oooooh!" The priestess danced round, threw the cock up and caught it by the neck.

"Prove yourself."

Then she broke its neck and threw it into the basin, whose water turned red immediately. If a pin had dropped, it would have been heard for the silence that fell upon all, for even the drummers were still.

Suddenly, a piercing scream filled the air, as the third wife broke out of the line. Her two children started crying, but no one looked at them as everyone gazed at the madwoman, confessing away.

"Yes! I killed him. I Erutaye, killed him!" She laughed hysterically as she threw her wrapper and headgear down, exposing her pink underwear-skirt.
"How will I not? He told me he would chase his useless wives away if I married him. I foolishly did and he tricked me! He kept them. He treated me like a mere concubine and demanded that I respect his wives. Echaibo! I thought if I poisoned his palm wine, I will be free to marry a young man that will treat me as number one. A whole me treated like a mistress. Echaibo!

Serves him right!" There was a mighty uproar as people began to stone and chase the fleeing mad woman.

"Next." The priestess called with apathy. A husband and wife pushed their possessed daughter through the crowd.

"Help us, oh mighty priestess of Agege." The man pleaded.

"Bring her forth!"

Same day.

The two women stood by the ariverbank. One woman wore plain old Ankara, with her wrapper tied loosely on her waist, she looked about, agitated, holding a black earthen plate containing blood. The other woman was dressed in a typical Igbe white wrapper, with a red cloth tied tightly around the waist and without the chalk make-up. She was in her seventies, forty years older than the other woman. She was shrinking and looked scary. Her eyes were dark and pure evil.

"If you do not calm down, I will drown you in this river." She coldly stated, still staring at the river.
"I'm just afraid. We ought to be at the festival, not at Agege river. You know they will match down here, as soon as the priestess finishes at the market square." The young woman with a tiny voice sighed. "Maybe I should have waited for the priestess at the square to bless me and the other women."

The old lady snickered. "Like she blessed you at last year's festival? And you wonder why you are still childless." She faced her. "Do you want a child or you want to remain childless when your husband's first, second, and fourth wives are springing eggs like a fat mother hen?" The lady bowed her head. "Emeteaworia, look at me when I'm talking to you. You asked for my help, I will do this my way, or you can wait for that fat pitiful slob, to pray for you again." She turned back to the river as Emeteaworia nodded for her to continue.

"Igugu" She called to the river. "The true goddess of the Igbes, your servants are here to require one of your many children. Here is your libation…" She collected the plate from Emeteaworia and poured its content into the river. "The blood of an Igbe maiden dancer. Bless your daughter, Emeteaworia, with a child, that she might no longer be a laughing stock among her fellow women, her husband can love her and in return, your children will continually come and pay homage to you."

She ground chalk in her palm, gave Emeteaworia little to eat and blew the rest into the river, then she turned to a stunning face.

"Is that it? No cock? No other sacrifices."

She smiled wickedly. "The blood of a human is higher than that of a cock, or goat. That is why we are better than that soft Agege priestess who calls herself a white witch." She slowly bent and picked some items from the ground.
"Take this Adjudju." She handed her a white hand fan with a round small mirror at its centre, a basin containing a small stool and a white native chalk. "Keep them for her, until she's big enough."

"A 'She'?" Emeteaworia looked at her hopefully, as she placed the basin on her head.

The old lady grinned, showing her sparse blackened teeth.
"Go. Before the white witches and villagers arrive here for their sacrifices."

Emeteaworia turned on her heels and hurried away while the old lady sang praises to Igugu Igbe, as she followed slowly behind.

CHAPTER ONE

December 1st 2010

New York, U.S.A.

"This is stupid."

Juanita sighed as she folded another piece of cloth into her red travelling bag. "This is the 9th time you're saying that. I know because I'm counting."

"Good" Craig huffed as he zipped his black travelling bag shut. "...because I intend to say it a few more times."

Juanita shut hers too and faced him. "Craig, I love you and all but sometimes I don't understand you. What is your problem?"

"My problem?" His American accent got louder. "I ain't got no problem babe. I'm just saying."

"What was that?"

"What?"

"You said 'ain't'."

 "So?"

"So a doctor –a highly educated one for that matter now talks ghetto, simply because he's going to see my mother?"

Craig held her gaze, then shrugged. "I'm a black American after all."

"Yeah, tell that to your high-classed black friends and watch them lynch you. Besides, your mother is white.

His eyes narrowed at her. "You are changing the subject."

Juanita giggled and turned away to straighten the bed. "I didn't know we were discussing any subject in particular."

"Yeah, right." He went into the bathroom to collect his shaving powder and other essential items. "You know" he called from the bathroom "this whole fuss is very unnecessary."

She massaged her temple with her right fingers. "Are you saying my mother is not important?"

Craig ignored her question. "Your mother is suffering from stress-related disorders. Her doctor said he wasn't entirely certain but she showed signs of obsessive-compulsive and post-traumatic stress disorder, resulting from abnormal responses to acute or prolonged anxiety." He sauntered into view. "At least she doesn't have Ebola or some other deadly disease roaming in Africa." He came close and stroked her dark Bob Marley braids. "We could stay back and let the good doctors over there, do their job. Or, better still, we could get her into the country. You rushing off and trying to ruin our careers, is not the answer. We would be obvious liabilities with nothing to do, but hold your mother's hand."

Juanita shifted, causing his hand to fall back to his side. She looked her fiancé over.
Craig was 31 years old and a neurosurgeon. He's been doing brain surgeries since he graduated from medical school, five years ago. He worked at Silver Hill Psychiatric Hospital in New Canaan, with other doctors like himself and like to think he was the best. Juanita didn't doubt he was good, but she certainly didn't believe he was even close to the best. But she let him dream on. Craig to her was the most handsome dude in the whole of America. His lips were so pink! Now, that is something he looks best in. His lips were his best assets, they lighted up his fair but really

tanned skin. He was 6feet 2inches tall and had a good body physique. With muscles displaying at all the right places. The problem was, he knew this.

Juanita frowned. "This stress-related disorders the doctor talked about, does it not mean my mum is going mad?"

"Well…"

"Did you not hear the doctor say, over the phone, that these disorders caused social phobias and depression for my mum, and could further cause suicidal idea?"

"Suicidal ideation."

"That's what I said." She snapped.

He raked his hands through his fried-curly hair –that was what Juanita called it. "Babe, all I'm saying is…"

"All you're saying…" She cut him off "is that I should abandon my mum, who has no one to care for her when she snaps in and out of the madness. Mind you, I haven't seen her in seven years. Seven solid years! You beat that. I believe we saw your rich mama last week talking about getting a tan in the Bahamas?"

"Fine." He wore his Italian shoes. "You are always good at taking words from my mouth. Let's go, boss. Let's travel half around the world to see your dear mother." He lifted his bag on his shoulder and bent to pick hers.

"Look, Craig…"

"Let's go. Our plane takes off in 20 minutes."

Juanita sighed as she closed the bedroom door and followed Craig through the living room. "You know what, sweet, you can stay if you want to."

Craig turned back angrily. "Don't you fucking 'sweet' me. I hate it when you call me that. And oh, you are terrific. I'm carrying our bags, I've taken leave from my important job and you say I can stay back? That isn't fucking cool!"

"You had better not use the 'F' word again." She growled.

"What? Don't swear, don't curse, don't talk ghetto…Juan, you are not my freaking mother!"

She massaged her temples. "I'm sorry for putting you through this. My job is important too, you know. And honestly, you could stay back because I don't know how much of your bitching I can take."

"Bitching." He shook his head and headed outside, towards his Porsche. "What an important job you have as an anti-trust lawyer." He snorted.

Juanita and Craig met five years ago at a bar mostly frequented by Tulane law students, in New Orleans. They were both in their final year and were attracted to each other at first sight. Juanita fell in love with his lips mostly and Craig later said he was attracted to her small pretty babyface. She was twenty-three years old then. Juanita was 5feet 6inches tall and loved wearing heels –well, maybe she'd wear it less if Craig wasn't so tall. They got engaged last year and decided to hold off the wedding so they could both get to the peak of their careers. Juanita was born and bred in Nigerian and moved to the States to complete her education. She presently worked in a firm of 300 lawyers and worked in the anti-trust department –which she hated of course. She'd rather be in litigations. Well, the firm said, literally, if she could work her butt off, for the years ahead, she might just make partner at 35. Let's not forget the emphasis on 'might'. She wasn't so sure she was going to be able to bill the required hours they demanded, since she had taken an indefinite leave, which her supervisor, of course, frowned at. She's been working there for 3 years and never had a leave, now she needed to take care of her mum, first leave ever, and they frown. Don't they have mothers? Juanita wondered as she buckled her seat belt in the plane, ignoring Craig who was still huffing and puffing.

*   *   *   *   *

12 hours later.

Nigeria. Murtala Muhammed Airport, Lagos.

"You see" Juanita spread her hands as they stepped out of the airport. Beautiful City. Civilized people speaking English. No barbarians prowling the City, hunting pretty foreigners like yourself."

"Were! Olosi Oloriburuku Omo ale." A taxi driver suddenly jumped out of his cab cursing a bike man who had swerved dangerously in front of him, in Yoruba tongue. "Koni da fun Iya laya e." He spread his ten fingers at the departing bike man.

Juanita looked at Craig's stunned face. "Oh well, just a few crazies. Besides, these are your brothers and sisters."

"No fucking way." He eyed the taxi driver who had now taken interest in them too. Resting his elbows against his wound-down window, he grinned, showing his tobacco-stained teeth.

"Ha, una welcome to Naija o. "He greeted in broken English. "Where una dey go?"

"Uh-oh." Juanita pulled Craig along and flagged another cab.

"Idiota" the taxi driver called out at them and zoomed off.

"I'm exhausted, Juan. When are we getting there?"

"I don't know."

"What?!"

"Keep your voice down!" She whispered as she looked around at the other passengers of the Siena, sandwiched together, headed for Kokori village. Most of them were already asleep, as it was half-past eleven at night.

"You said it would be like an adventure." He said accusingly.

"Give me a break, Craig. First of all, I didn't know she had been taken to the village, why in heavens they would do that, I don't know. You were there when I called her phone and her nurse picked. I have never been to the village before, so I'm not used to it too. As soon as I see my mum, we'll move back to Lagos City and make travel arrangements for her to return with us to the States. Then we can all go back to our normal lives."
The car stopped and everyone got out.

"Now what?" Craig frowned at the dirty environment, where bikes were carrying people off.
A dark woman with braided hair and Ankara locally made skirt and blouse, approached them.

"Miss Juanita?"

"Oh, yes. Er- are you, Simbi? My mum's nurse?"

She nodded. "Yes. I'm sorry, your journey must have really been stressful. Welcome to Kokori." She did not smile. Juanita nodded, Craig just frowned. "Please come, our transport is waiting."

When Craig saw the three bike men, he stopped walking.

"Hell. No way I'm getting on that."

Simbi smiled faintly. "I am sorry, it is all we can get at this time of the night. If you prefer to walk, you will be ambushed before you get halfway."
They finally got on each of the rickety bikes, behind its riders and rode off.

"Thank God, there's light here," Juanita said as she followed Simbi into a compound, housing a small bungalow. "it was so dark all the way here."

"It is generator," Simbi said. "the light is bad again, but when they finally repair it, you will enjoy it for long."

They entered the parlour and Juanita wasn't quite shocked to see five elderly men looking gravely at her. She knew why. She had sensed it ever since Simbi showed up. She was so tired she couldn't deal with this right now. She realized she was slipping to the floor and the last thing she remembered was Craig catching her and calling out her name.

CHAPTER TWO

"What the fuck do you mean, she's dead? How can she be fucking dead when I spoke with her two days ago!" Exclaimed Juanita.

She had woken up some minutes before three in the morning to find herself on bed, with Craig, in a room full of her mum's clothes and other possessions. She remembered the five men that had been sitting in her mother's parlour before she fainted. She sprung out of the room to find them sprawled about, sleeping in the parlour. She had screamed for them to wake up and Craig hurriedly joined her in his pyjamas, Simbi also rushed out of her room, securing her wrapper under her armpit. One of the men, the eldest among them, who looked to be in his eighties, fanned himself with his black hat, then broke the news of her mother's death, as calmly as he could.

"What the bloody hell happened? Can someone speak, goddammit!"

"Er —honey?" Craig lifted a finger uncertainly.

"Yes, sugar?" She spat back. Her eyes blazing with fury.

"It's just that y-you are cursing. You know how you feel about using such languages, as a learned…"

Juanita's hysteric laughter cut him off. "And you think I give a shit about my language right now, Craig? Is that the only godforsaken thing that popped into your head? My freaking language in freaking public?"

"It's not like that, I'm just trying to help…"

"You." She pointed a finger at the cowering Simbi. "Start talking. And you better have a good explanation as to why you brought my mother from the City to this dump!" Three of the elders winced.

Simbi's bottom lips trembled.

"It –it's not my doing. Mama said I must bring her to the village and your mother was really worse, I didn't know what to do."

"You didn't know what to do? Who hired you, 'cause it sure wasn't me. I know, Dr Olatunde Bamiloye, and if he had any part in this, I'm suing him. I will sue his bloody hospital, I will sue you!"

"Hah," Simbi fidgeted. "Ma, I only followed orders o. Your mother had gone mad. Mama had to send men from the village to carry her from Lagos, from the gutter she had been sitting in. The doctor had no choice but to give consent because he couldn't control it, he sent me to tag along, just in case. The drugs I was giving her weren't even working."

"Mama. Who the hell is this Mama making all the decisions... to bring my mother to a place with no adequate medical treatment? My mo-" Her voice broke. "My mother went mad and you didn't tell me?" Tears ran down both cheeks, blurring her vision, she wiped furiously at it, so she could see the shame-faced nurse clearly.

"It happened the day before yesterday!" Simbi tried to defend herself, as she began to cry too. "If you were here, you couldn't have thought straight. I could not control her, she went violent, slamming her head into glass doors, speaking with strange voices that were clearly not hers. Mama happened to call at that moment, and while I was on the phone, she escaped outside. I told mama I had to follow her and said she was sending people over to get her. It took them over five hours to get to Lagos, and I had just found her sitting quietly in a gutter. I called Doctor and he told me to follow them back with Madam, to the village. She was calm all the way, but as soon as we got to the village, she –she started murmuring and when the car stopped in this compound, she won't come out. She started crying. Mama came out and all was well again. She became normal. Talked normal. Mama said her Pastor was going to handle it, that it was not a medical matter and that her enemies would not succeed in taking her daughter. Honestly, if you had seen Madam displaying, you would know it was a spiritual attack. The Pastor came yesterday and when we looked for Madam, we couldn't find her. We later found her by the bank of a river..." she paused "...dead."

Juanita collapsed into a brown worn-out sofa.

"Who –who is this Mama?" She managed to ask, with her head buried between her knees.

"Omome, welcome." (Omome meant, my child).

Juanita lifted her head slowly to look at the old woman, with a tiny voice but piercing dark eyes that seemed to bore holes into her very soul. Her mother's eyes. Oh my God, her grandmother! How could she-? She had forgotten her.

"Nana?"

The old lady smiled sadly, as she shuffled slowly forward. She was bent over and wouldn't take her eyes off Juanita.

"Alas, my enemies have won. They have taken my daughter." Tears streamed down her shrewd face. She was a small woman, Juanita thought. Her grandma put her trembling palms on Juanita's cheeks. "Go. Go from here. Go back to the foreign land you came from."

Juanita's face crumpled. "Nana, how can you say that now? I'm sorry I forgot you. I haven't seen or heard about you since I was maybe five? You never visited us in the City, and mum never talked about you with me. Forgive me. Mum is gone. That stupid doctor and his nurse killed her. But Nana, why did you bring her here? I was planning to fly her to America with me, where she would get better treatment. He's a doctor too." She pointed at Craig, sitting on the edge of her couch. Everyone turned to look at him as if they had just noticed someone else was there. He frowned at his toes.

"Never mind." She continued. "I won't blame you for your ignorance if you don't punish me for not keeping in touch with you." She burst into tears and rested on the frail woman's bosom. Nana tried to support her, but they both crumbled on the red rug, weeping and hugging.

"Oh Omome, my dear ignorant and innocent child, what an old man see while seated, the young cannot see even from a mountain top. You should not have come."

CHAPTER THREE

"My child."

Juanita opened her eyes. Wasn't that her mother's voice?

"Mum?" She looked about her and her eyes widened at her darkened environment. She could see she was nowhere she recognized...sitting on a big stone, all alone on a bushy deserted road.

"Hello? Where in god's name am I?"

"My poor baby. Come."

Juanita looked about her but could see no one. "Mum? Where are you?" She stood up and wrapped her arms about herself to shield her body from the freezing weather. The trees began to shake violently and the wind blew at her white skirt. "Mum, I can't see you. And I'm scared."

"Over here."

Juanita suddenly saw her. She was tying a white wrapper, with a basin on her head, standing by the river bank. Weird, Juanita thought. Her mum looked like a typical villager. And she could swear she had looked ahead before and that river had not been there.

"Come." Her mother said, stretching her right hand towards her. God, her mother was a beautiful woman, had her long hair grown to her waist or was it a weave-on? Her fair skin was almost white and her long finger and toenails were painted white. Juanita started towards her, mesmerized.

Then she frowned. Had her mother moved into the water or was it her imagination? Sure enough, as she moved closer, her mother moved farther into the river.

"Mum, stop, you know you can't swim!"

Her mum smiled sadly and kept moving backwards with her hands still outstretched. "No one tests the depth of a river with both feet."

"I said stop!" Juanita began to run.

Her mother looked about the water, which had risen to her chest. Then at her daughter. "Come my child, hurry!" She shrieked in fear. But it was too late, the water swallowed her as Juanita reached the river bank.

"Mummy!" She screamed as her mother's right hand disappeared into the water.

"Omome, wake up."

Juanita opened her eyes slowly. "Mum?"

"Poor child." Nana touched her cheek. "You have had an evening-mare."

"It's a nightmare, Nana," Craig said, amused.

"It is not yet night." She retorted.

"You have my mother's eyes," Juanita said.

"You too." Nana helped her seat up. "Are you well?"

She placed her head on Craig's lap. He was sitting on the arm of the long brown cushion she had fallen asleep upon. "How long have I been asleep?"

Craig shrugged. "A couple of hours."

"Come to the dining table, my children. You will need your strength." Nana led the way.

"I'm not sure my stomach can take anything right now." But Juanita let Craig support her to the dining table, to a boring plate of Ogwo soup and starch. If only they weren't under these circumstances, she'd have probably enjoyed eating this local dish. But right now, it tasted like sandpaper on her tongue. Simbi came out from her room and spied them eating, she stood looking down as they spotted her.

"I –I'm leaving." She said quietly, heaving her blue travelling bag upon her right shoulder. "I'm taking the night bus."

"What? You couldn't wait to get rid of your late patient's family?" Silence.

"I –It's not like that." She almost whispered. "I have a job to keep."

Juanita sighed and rose up. "I'll see you off."

"Oh, that is not necessary…"

"I insist." She washed her hands in the washing bowl provided on the table and followed the reluctant Simbi outside.

"I'm supposed to take a bike to town, where I'll find a car park."

"We'll walk a bit. If you get tired of carrying your bag, we could stop and sit somewhere. I just need to know –or at least understand what happened to my mum. I knew she was partially insane…but you said 'mad' like you really meant 'mad'.

"She reminded me of the man in the bible, with the legions of demons in him." Simbi shuddered.

Juanita screwed her face disapprovingly. "Aren't you exaggerating just a little bit?"

"No." Simbi stopped on her heels, causing Juanita to stumble behind her. "I have seen mad people." She said, staring up into Juanita's eyes, as she was shorter. "Your mother wasn't just mad, she was possessed. By a very powerful demon at that."

Now Juanita shuddered. "Look, I don't believe in this African voodoo mentality that…"

"African voodoo mentality?" Simbi gaped at her. "Your mother spoke in strange voices, lifted up the freezer and single-handedly hauled it against the window, smashed her head and hands into glass, feeling no pain and possessing the strength of ten men and you say voodoo mentality?" She shook her head irritably.
"You people, you leave the country and live like foreigners, forgetting your root and foundation. Oga o."

Juanita stopped and sat on the wood of a fallen tree, beside the road, looking at passersby but not really seeing them. Simbi dropped her bag and sat too.

"I work at Horizon Hospital, owned by Dr Olatunde Bamiloye. Your mum had always been a patient, in the hospital. She did all her check-up with us and we've been treating her for stress and high blood pressure. Things changed dramatically in April. I'm sure it began on April 1st, because she came in that day to complain that she couldn't sleep. We started treating her Insomnia, but it got worse. Madam Ovore was worried that her journey to the village had caused it. But then we couldn't see how. Anyway, you were aware of the progressive stage of her ailment, and in August, I was assigned to move in with her. It turned out she had gone back to the village, but her case had gotten worse when she returned. She told me voices were speaking to her. She told me she was twice ordered to pick things from inside the toilet and swallow.

"Wait" Juanita interrupted. "Swallow what?"

"I don't know. I was too scared to ask. I'm not even sure she knew what it was either. Some days she was hysteric, screaming about shadows and voices and how your Father was a wizard and had initiated her only child into his evil cult…"

"What?"

"Hmm. They are too numerous to remember. But one account I will never forget, was when her pastor came to visit. She used to be a prayer warrior in church but had completely withdrawn. The pastor had come to discuss her faith and how her lack of service to God was the reason for her problems and the fall of her business." Simbi snickered. "Even I knew it was not so. As fate would have it, that tormenting spirit came upon Madam Ovore before the Pastor could leave. He started binding and casting and I was really hopeful that the evil spirit would leave her, after all. Then a male voice spoke through her and told the pastor to mind his own business that she was his. He called his name when the pastor demanded it, but I don't remember, I was busy listening to the next voice, she sounded like a lady of great authority and called Madam her offspring. While the pastor continued to pray, another voice spoke." Simbi paused and looked at Juanita.

"She introduced herself as Emetetiabo. She was crying and begging everybody, including the spirits, to leave her daughter alone for her." She exhaled heavily. "I could not forget that name." She continued. "I took interest in the voice, because I recognized it as the woman who called from the village and said she was Madam Ovore's Mama."
Juanita was dumbfounded. Simbi rose up and lifted her bag.
"I have to run. I do not want to wait around to find out why all the prayers of the many pastors and churches your mother kept running to, could not deliver her." She started to leave but turned on second thought.

"Go back to your fantasy land, while you still can." She walked away, leaving Juanita, who still didn't know what to say.

*　　　*　　　*　　　*　　　*

Juanita started to walk back to her mother's house, when she was accosted by two young ladies, her age, buying groundnut from a small kiosk owned by a Hausa man.

"Hi!" The one with a big bosom and heavy make-up, greeted her, trying to sound foreign without success...is that a black dot pasted on her forehead?

"Hi," Juanita replied coolly.

"I heard your mother, mad." Big bosom said.

Juanita flinched and saw a man who had hurriedly been rolling a wheelbarrow filled with firewoods, averting his face as if he hadn't wanted to be seen, suddenly stopped. Juanita was sure he had heard the loud-mouth because he turned and crossed the street pushing the wheelbarrow before him.

"Ikebe." He called to the big bosom.

"Pastor." Ikebe's face lit up. Pastor? Juanita looked at the man who was in his early thirties, dressed in brown trousers rolled up to the knee, his bathroom slippers had chopped off at the back, his shirt was brown or was it cream? You couldn't tell, really. His beard looked a week old and his eyes...like honey. The eyes were staring right back at her with amusement. The good thing about blushing when you are not white is that no pink colour surfaces on your cheeks, so he probably didn't know she was abashed at being caught staring at him. Or did he? With the half-smile on his face, one couldn't really tell. Do illiterates know these things?

"Pastor." The other over-weight lady mumbled shyly.

"How are you, Oke?"

Okay, he was no illiterate. Juanita concluded at his neat Nigerian accent, with a deep drawling voice.
"F –fine." Oke looked at her feet. Ikebe was bolder. She planted herself between the wheelbarrow and Pastor.

"Which message you are about? Can I help you?"

"Er –em. Hello." He shifted backwards and turned to Juanita. "I'm sorry about your mother and ladies..." He turned to the other females, with a stern look on his face. "The way you spoke earlier to the Miss, was wrong for someone who just lost her mother. You should apologize."

They stared blankly at him.
"Say sorry."

Understanding dawned on their faces, and together they chorused "Sorry."

Juanita was even more embarrassed, but she managed to smile.

"It's okay. If you'll excuse me." She could tell the pastor guy wanted to speak to her, as she hurried off, but Ikebe was already harassing him with her chest and asking questions like…when are you marrying…?

When Juanita got home, she found her grandma in the kitchen. She had a wistful look on her face, with tears running down both eyes.

"Nana." She called quietly, tears threatening to fall down her own eyes as she sat on a stool.

Nana wiped her tears off with her wrapper and started to put on the stove. "When are you leaving? She asked, almost coldly.

Juanita frowned at her. "I don't know."

"Your husband wants to go back."

She didn't bother to correct her. Nana knew they weren't married anyway. "We will, after the burial."

"Good." The room had gone silent but for the crackling stove. Nana began to peel yam in the sink. "What?" She asked quietly.

"What is your name?" Silence. "Nana?"

"Why do you ask now?" Nana did not turn to look at her.

"I just want to know." Silence. "Nana?"

"Emetetiabo."

CHAPTER FOUR

It took a whole week for the burial ceremony to hold. Her mother had been a rich woman, at least, before her business collapsed and she came into debt. She used to sell Ankara, Hollandice, George and other expensive clothing materials in Lagos. Some of her fellow business women had come today for the burial. One had even asked Juanita if it were possible to get back the N150,000 she had borrowed her mother. Juanita had in turn, viciously explained the term 'bad debt' to her and the other cowering ladies. Juanita met her mum's stepbrothers and sisters. Most of which were villagers and kept greeting her 'doh' (sorry). Their Ankara was patterned blue but sowed in different styles. Craig wore the Ankara too, but Juanita as the first and only child of her mum was conformed to where a George, which was a white lace blouse with big puffy shoulders and equally big tied double purple wrappers around her waist.

Craig hung his nose up as if his native attire stunk, but he couldn't complain, not to Juanita in her mood. He was tired of the village and the mosquitoes. He feared he might die if he fell ill here. The service was conducted by Nana's pastor, in which a lot of people cried for the early departure of a 40-year-old woman. After he left, the relatives took over, with the live band invited, playing. It was like a party as they shared food and drinks. Finally, around 10:00 pm, Juanita greeted the last family member, locked her mother's gate and went inside the house. She fell straight on top her bed and began to snore, without noticing Craig who had been waiting for her by the window, wearing only his native trouser.

Craig stepped outside the next morning to find Juanita sitting in front of her mother's grave at the porch. A man had been hired to come in this morning and tile the grave. She was with a stainless tray of melon. "What a tradition…that tells you to bury the dead inside the house people live in, just so rain doesn't beat them." Juanita muttered to no one in particular. "I mean, they are dead, for crying out loud."

"What are you doing?" He sat beside her on the long bench.

"Picking shafts from the melon." She smiled at him. "I had forgotten how to do this. You wanna try?" She offered him the tray.

"Where the Oyinbo?"

Juanita looked up to see Ikebe leading a group of about ten people, including her fat friend, towards them.

"Wado ooh." She and the others greeted, peering about as if they were looking for someone. "We hear say you come with Oyinbo." Ikebe, the spokesperson, excitedly, began to lead her entourage inside.

"Wait!" Juanita held back the laughter bubbling inside of her. "When you say Oyinbo…you mean a foreigner, right?"

They exchanged glances. "Yes…" Ikebe said uncertainly. "White man."

"This is him." She pointed at Craig, who looked like he was about to flee.

"This no be Oyinbo na!" The youngest boy of about fourteen shouted, looking affronted. "Me know Oyinbo."

Juanita giggled. "Oh, his mother is white. He is Oyinbo. Say something." She nudged him.

"Um –I –er –I'm an American. My name's Craig."

"You hear wetin him talk?" The boy asked the others.

"He just say shrewy shrewy shrewy," Oke confirmed.

"Pastor even fine pass am, sef." Ikebe eyed him. "This one na Naija guy na."

"Abeg, make we they go." Another female dressed in shorts and a bandana tied on her forehead started to bounce away, with the others tagging along.

"Em…sorry, for your mother," Ikebe said, as an afterthought.

"Sorry o." The others chorused and left. Juanita burst into laughter as soon as they were out of sight.

"Oh, that was fun! They think you're a Nigerian. You are not Oyinbo. Haha!"

"Yea…haha." Craig croaked. "Can we leave now?" Craig got up abruptly, causing the bench to rock, nearly knocking Juanita off it. "Our business here is over."

"I need to talk to Nana first." Juanita looked at the grave, all trace of humour gone.

"Well, then go do that now, so we can leave tomorrow."

"Yes," Nana said, as she stepped out. "Let us talk so you can leave tomorrow."

"Excuse me." Craig walked back inside the house.

The silence between them got a tad uncomfortable before Juanita spoke up.

"What happened to my mother?" Just as Juanita was getting impatient for the lack of response…

"My enemies took her."

"What enemies?"

Nana looked her in the eyes. "People in this village were jealous of my beautiful rich daughter. Even your Father."

"And you're saying they just killed her?"

"Yes."

Juanita stood up and began to pace. "I don't believe you. What are you hiding from me? You know more than you're letting on!"

Nana got up and held her cheeks in both hands. "My child, leave this place before they take you from me."

"Why? Juanita was getting hysterical. "Tell me why anyone would want to take me!"

"Some things are better left unsaid. It is true that what you do not know, cannot kill you…"

A peal of wicked laughter filled the air. Both Nana and Juanita turned to see a young beautiful lady in white Buba, stand a few feet from them.

"Emetetiabo, you of all people know that is not true. I mean, look at your daughter…" She pointed at the grave. Juanita didn't notice Nana shiver as she sat shakily on the bench. She was too busy wondering what word to use in shutting this disrespectful woman up.

"Go," Nana said to her. "leave this village. Go back to the foreign land and never come back."

"Yes, go." The young lady sneered as she cat-walked closer to Nana. "But you will surely come back. The Chickens always return to Mother Hen."

"Look here woman…" Juanita began.

"I said get out of here. Pack and leave me alone!" Nana screamed with all her strength.

Dazed, Juanita stumbled hurriedly, inside. What had just happened? Who was that woman? Maybe she should leave, she wasn't sure she wanted to know why a young lady would talk to her grandma's age in that manner, exuding so much confidence. And the lady knew who she was. Something diabolic was in play here. Did she have to know? Would knowing bring her mother back?

"Craig, we are leaving right now." She said as she burst into the room.

"About time."

CHAPTER FIVE

Dec. 12th

Asaba, Delta State.

"Did you get the tickets?" Craig asked, as soon as Juanita entered their hotel room.

"To Lagos, yes. In one hour." She dumped her brown purse on the rocky chair, kicked off her brown flat sandals and laid on the bed, closing her eyes…

"To Lagos?" Craig swivelled on the bed to look at her face.

"We'd get another flight out of the country from there."

Craig wanted to complain but decided against it. "Why aren't you excited about it, then?" He pulled her reluctant body into his arms. "Okay, come on, let's go sightseeing before we travel. This place is after all more civilized than the village…"

"I'm not in the mood, Craig. Maybe you should pack."

"Pack what? We didn't unpack" He gestured at their bags right at the corner of the white-painted room, they had lodged in, since arriving from Kokori by public bus. The room was drab and lacked any major design, just a single bed, a top to bottom wardrobe and a rocky chair. At least, it didn't cost much, especially for someone paying in dollars.

"What do we do then, while we wait? I'm bored."

She closed her eyes tight and massaged her temples. "I don't know, Craig dear." She said with an effort. "Watch T.V or something."

Juanita turned her face into the pillow, as she thought about her events that day. This morning they had left her mother's house, with Nana and the young lady on white, watching them go. As they walked, arguing about whether there was an alternative, aside from a bike, to take them to the park…she saw that Pastor, whose name she didn't know, chatting with the Hausa man, outside his kiosk. As soon as he saw them, he stopped talking, with the groundnut he was holding, halfway to his mouth. Juanita averted her eyes, so she didn't see him wave a hand in greeting. But that wasn't what spooked her. They had just gotten to the park when someone grabbed her left free hand. But turning back, she saw a mad man.

"Holy shit!" She had snatched her hand away from his, but he just smiled at her palm, then her face and walked away.

"What was that about?" Craig had asked, aghast.

"Beats me."

Juanita frowned and raised her head from the pillow, as she heard Craig's voice.

"No, no, no, no. Juan, tell me that's not the same airport we are boarding our flight."

She turned her attention to the T.V, she didn't realize Craig had switched it on. A reporter was standing a few feet away from the Asaba Airport, with a raging fire behind and firemen running back and forth to quench the fire.

"...the Aero Contractors crashed into the runway, for reasons yet to be ascertained, damaging over 9000 feet of the runway. Two passengers on board, have been confirmed dead and the number of injured has risen to eleven, still counting, as rescue teams have been deployed to get them all out of the burning plane. Mr Omotoba Chris, the Minister of Aviation, is on his way to Asaba as we speak..."

 "Is it?" Craig raised his voice over the reporter's, while pointing at the television.

"Yes," Juanita whispered, her eyes glued to the screen.

"What do we do now? Can we still travel, I mean it's not the same plane..."

"...due to the damaged plane on the runway, all flight has been cancelled indefinitely...this is the breaking news coming to you live from Silverbird Television, Asaba, I'm Otega Rachel..."

"Dammit to hell!" Craig flung the remote against the T.V as if to hit the reporter.

"Calm down, Craig! There will be other ways."

"What other way? I am not taking public transport and seating for six hours, sandwiched among smelly people."

"Jesus, Craig. You're so insensitive." Juanita sat up. "Here I am, trying to please you and leave the country, as you wished. But have you shown any sympathy towards the loss of my mother? Do you even realize I'm mourning? Hell, people just lost their lives on that plane and all you can think of, is your delayed trip."

"I will be in mourning too if I lose my job." He said, unrepentant. "And if I didn't care for you, I won't be here. How many men do you think would travel halfway around the world for a woman, just so she could mourn?"

"Definitely not men like you." She placed her head on the table and began watching the cartoon, Tom and Jerry.
"Do not worry." She smirked at Craig who had a frustrated look on his face, as he watched Tom chase Jerry. "We'd get a private taxi to drive us to Lagos on 150km per hour."

*   *   *   *   *

12:00am

The drums got louder in her head. She turned left on the bed, then right. The more she turned, the louder it got. Now, she could hear the voices of women shouting, she couldn't stand it anymore, so she opened her eyes.

"Juanita!"

She turned sharply to see a lady in her mid-thirties, dressed in white wrapper and red beads on her waist, dancing and beckoning for her to join her.

"We are headed to the river…" She said, not missing her step as she pointed to the other females on white ahead, dancing vigorously with basins on their heads.

Juanita looked about the dark road, as she moved closer to the one who had called her.

"Don't I know you?"

She rolled her eyes. "I am your mother's step-sister, Dinah. You saw me at the burial… take." A basin suddenly materialized on her outstretched palm, causing Juanita to stumble backwards in shock.

"How did you do…?"

"It belongs to you now." She smiled at Juanita.

"What's in it?" Juanita asked uncertainly.

"Your property to worship Igbe."

Juanita chuckled. "What? Will Nigeria ever stop this fetish stuff? I mean, we are in a new age now. No such thing as gods. You need to wake up to the modernized world."

Dina just stared at her. "It is your turn. The time has come." She had stopped dancing.

Juanita massaged her temples. "I told you, I don't want it."

Dina laughed in her face. "You do not have a choice."

Juanita stared her down. "Yes, I do. I'm leaving this sick family I'm surrounded by and returning to the States."

"You can't!"

"Watch me!" Juanita turned defiantly and started off, but she slipped.

Juanita opened her eyes and found herself hanging by the rails of the balcony of their hotel room. She looked down, then screamed as she fell down the one-storey building.

Craig was seated at the waiting area, with his head buried in his arms, when someone touched his shoulders. He raised his head to see a very beautiful, light-skinned nurse, with the deepest silver eyes he had ever seen. She looked like a goddess. She smiled at him as if to say 'I know you think I'm beautiful.'

"You are not her husband." She said.

Craig came back to earth. "Pardon?"

"The patient you and the hotel brought in this morning."

"Oh, yeah. She's my fiancée."

"She is not yours."

"I beg your pardon?" Craig looked at her, confused. What was she talking about?

"You are weaving around the tarantula's sacred web and this will cause his fangs to inflict untold pain on you."

"What the…"

"She is married, already. Go back to your world…while you still can." She winked at him, turned and cat-walked out of the hospital, leaving an open-mouthed Craig to stare at the empty double doors. He shuddered, as he hurried to Juanita's room. When he got there, he found her awake.

"Hey." She smiled weakly at him.

"Hey." He looked and pointed at her legs. "Your legs…"

"Fine. Miraculously, nothing's broken, just sprained. This is so because I fell on the inflated pool bed. Only God knows what would have become of me if I had fallen on the gravel."

Craig sat on the bed thoughtfully. "You can't travel today."

Juanita sighed. "Apparently not. I'm so sorry, baby. The doctor said they needed to monitor my high blood pressure, due to the shock I got into."

"Isn't this your mother all over again?" Craig asked, abruptly.

"What?"

"Think about it." Craig stood up and began to pace the floors of the white private room. "Shock, disorders, high blood pressure…"

"I'm not going mad, Craig." She said coldly.

"Aren't you?" He stopped at the feet of the springy bed. "You got up at the middle of the night and the next thing, you are hanging by the railing outside. What were you doing there?"

"I had a nightmare! I –sort of sleep-walked…, I don't know." She rubbed her forehead.

"This is too much for me, Juan. I didn't bargain for this." He raked his hands through his hair. "Tell you what…" He said, turning away from her. "Why don't I travel, then when you're fit, you can come and join me at home? I –I'll be waiting for you."

Coward. Juanita shook her head at his back. "Fine Craig, go."

"Really?" He turned too fast. "I mean, okay…if it's alright with you." He tried to act calmly. "I would make everything ready for your arrival…"

"Don't bother your pretty head, dear. This relationship is over." She said coolly.

Craig paused, then chuckled. "Why? Because I don't want to be in your country? Is that a crime?"

"No, sweetie pie." She sneered. "It's because you care about no one but yourself."

"I could say the same about you!" He spat angrily. "Dragging me all the way, for your sorry excuse of a family's sake!" He clenched his fist. "I didn't mean it like that…"

"Just go, Craig. You are entitled to your own opinion about my family. Get out of my life. I know that's what you really want to do." She pointed a finger, accusatorily, at him. "You are just too chicken to do it, so I'm helping you. Take it now and leave with some dignity, if you have any left."

"Fine, fine. Goodbye, Juan. It was fun while it lasted…"

"Get out!" Craig gave her one last look and stormed out, slamming the door behind him.

CHAPTER SIX

Nana couldn't continue. She dropped the basin she had been carrying on her head and leaned heavily on her walking stick. She was too old for this. Why wouldn't they let her die in peace? Why couldn't she be a normal grandma surrounded by children? Why did she have to be trekking a lonely forest by twelve in the hot afternoon? Maybe she should die here, yes. But even death won't stop the problems, would it? Her lineage was about to be wiped out. Her last ray of light was about to be extinguished by the same monsters who gave her the light. Oh, it is true what they say, she shook her head in regret…if you collect a hand from the devil, he would not only take the hand back but your leg too. Yes, she should die. Peradventure, she'd make it to heaven...

"Mama, let me help you." She jumped at the sight of the boy, no more than twelve, who had suddenly materialized at her side, speaking in their native dialect.

She laughed bitterly. "You people will not even let me die?"
The boy picked up the basin and started moving ahead of her, turning every now and then to make sure she was following.

Nana entered the shrine. It was just an abandoned dilapidating brick house. The roof was old and rusted, with gaping holes here and there. The place was infested by lizards, wall geckos, soldier ants, big black mosquitoes and other insects she couldn't name. The bushes around hugged the walls whose original colour could not be told. Though it looked like it had been red. The boy stopped, dropped the basin and entered an inner room, with red curtains, representing the door. The young lady who visited her unannounced was seated on the earthen ground, with legs crossed (Muslim style), hands outstretched in prayers and eyes closed.

"Welcome, Emetetiabo."

She dropped the basin and sat opposite the priestess.

"I have come to make sacrifices on behalf of my grand-daughter." She said confidently.

The Priestess's eyes flew open and she laughed most wickedly. "You are a joker, old woman!"

"I want to speak to your grandma!" She replied defiantly. "You are just a small girl, who's had too much power thrust into her little fingers. When the head is too big, it cannot dodge blows."

The priestess pupils turned red with fury as she slammed both palms on the hard ground.

"If a mouse must make jest of a cat, then it must also find a hole nearby. Call me 'small' one more time." She growled in a thousand voices.

Nana shivered involuntarily. "I wish to speak to your grandma." She insisted.

"Very well." The priestess spoke in her normal voice. "You will have your wish." She closed her eyes, lifted a boiling earthen pot from the stove made from firewoods, and placed it in front of her. Nana marvelled that she had not been burnt, lifting the pot like it was water from the fridge. She started to chant in strange tongues and the pot before her, began to boil furiously, then it spilt. But instead of spilling hot water, the air was filled with thick smoke blurring Nana's vision of the priestess.

"Emetetiabo." A cold familiar voice spoke through the priestess.

"Great priestess!" Nana breathed in relief. "I need your help. Your granddaughter is mean. She is much wicked than the devil himself. She and her fellow witches have killed my daughter and now they are after my last hope...my granddaughter! Help me!"

A burst of formidable laughter filled the air. "Help you? A person who begs for food is an insult to a generous farmer. What happened to the new god you have been serving? Are you not a Christian anymore?

Nana fidgeted. "Of course I am. But they do not understand these things. Let me pay one last sacrifice to Igbe and leave, so I can make heaven. I don't want to go to hell. Look..." She pointed to the basin. "I have come with my daughter's basin. If I do this, you'd spare her life, enh...children are the reward of life."

"You fool!" The voice was angry. "Were you not there when we required a child from the great goddess? Did you not know that your daughter and all her offspring to come, generation to generation, belonged to Igugu Igbe?" The voice thundered. "Were you not there when we said her children must return to pay homage and give sacrifice unto her? Did you not know that your offspring were married off to the god of the river? You ignorant fool! If I were in the land of the living, I would have slapped your old haggard face! You say you lost a daughter? Did I not lose mine when the idiot became a Christian, thinking she could run from her destiny? If you rattle a snake, you should be prepared to be beaten by it. Call your grandchild to order before she suffers her mother's fate. For the great waters are angry and the sanction has already begun!" With that, the atmosphere cleared, and the priestess opened her eyes.

"D –does that mean I can't offer the sacrifice on her behalf?" Nana asked dejectedly.

The priestess smiled menacingly. "And you thought I was much wicked than the devil."

"W –what did she mean by the sanction has already begun?"

"You know what it means." She sneered at Nana's frightened face. "The day before yesterday, your granddaughter nearly fell to her death. That was just a minor warning. The next will not be so pleasant." Nana could smell her foul breath of rotten eggs, as she thrusts her face so close to hers.
"She cannot leave. We are doing her a favour by keeping her here and giving her a chance to return. The moment we let her go and she returns to the foreign land, we will strike her. No matter how far, we are connected by blood. And the sheep that refuses to stay with the flock will be prey for the teeth of the wolf."

*   *   *   *   *

Nana could still hear the priestess voice in her head, as she howled in laughter, while she was leaving. She had taken a bend at a crossroad in the forest, headed for another shrine. This was what she should have done so many years ago. She should have allowed the white witch to bless her with children. But wouldn't they have wanted to control her daughter's life too? To take it when they deemed fit? She got to the shrine. This one was made of red mud and bamboos for the roof, but it was neat. Some children playing nude in front of the hut stopped their game of 'Zozozo' and stared at her. She stared back at their tiny bodies, with a scraped head for both boys and girls and powder all over their necks.

"Where is your grandma?" Or was she a great-grandma? Nana wondered as she asked them in the native tongue. A little girl of about five ran into the hut, while the others just stared at her, without blinking. The girl returned and gestured for her to go in. Nana stooped even lower than her already bent form, to enter the hut.

An old over-weight woman lay on a mat on the bare but clean floor. The room had a makeshift wardrobe, where her clothes hung and so many mirrors resting against the wall. Other than the table with a plate of Usi and Banga soup, the room was bare.

"What brings you here?" The old priestess asked without sitting up.

"You don't know me…" Nana started.

"I know you are one of the rebel children of the great one." She sat up with much effort. "I know everything."

Nana sighed. "If you knew, then you must know why I'm here."

She shook her head pitifully. "Rain beats a leopard's skin, but it doesn't wash out the spots. You sort for a child from the enemy of Agege Igbe and you got one. Why do you want us to help you keep the property of Igugu Igbe?

"Mighty priestess, I made a terrible mistake. I should have waited for your blessings but I was desperate…"

"And you went to the devil herself!" The priestess snapped. "We used to be one, before she and her entourage broke off, to seek the darker power of the rebellious sister of Agege Igbe. You made a pact with them and became one of Igugu Igbe's followers. By doing this, you renounced us, their mark and spot are on your generation. There is nothing I can do for you."

"Please. Let me offer sacrifices to the true god of the Igbes if she would show mercy for my stupidity and save my grandchild. She is all I have left and those demons have evoked their sanction on her already!"

The priestess sighed. "The white witches are not evil. Our god forgives. Let me pray to the goddess and hear what she says concerning your grandchild. There is always a solution. Go, and come back in the next market day. I will have an answer then."

"Thank you, thank you." She carried the basin and tried her best to hurry out.

CHAPTER SEVEN

Dec. 17th 7:02am

Asaba, Delta State.

Juanita paid her transport fare at the counter of Agofure motors, collected her ticket, thanked the smiling girl behind the counter and then dragged her red travelling bag to the lounge to await her bus. She was going to Lagos. She would just see her father briefly, then head back to the states, where she rightly belonged. As she made herself comfortable on the wooden chair, she recalled her conversation with her dad, when she called him last night, for lack of no one else to talk to.

"How are you?" He had asked distantly.

"Fine. And you?"

"Fine. Very fine."

"Em, and your wife and kids?"

"They are fine. We thank God. Really fine."

"Fine..." Juanita had slapped herself mentally. Were they going to stop with the 'Fine'? "So...I just wanted to check on you. I'm in the country."

"I know...judging from your phone number."

"And you know mum, I mean, my mum is gone?" She couldn't help but ask.

There was a long silence before he replied. "Yes."

"And you couldn't even attend her funeral? Did you hate her that much?"

Her father sighed heavily over the phone. "Juan love..."

"You have a new family now. I'm not your love." She said coldly, wiping a tear that had slipped down her face. "I just wanted you to know that I'm still alive and I was just discharged from the hospital. I'll be travelling back." Pause.

"Why don't you come to see me in Lagos before you leave? Are you alright? What happened?"

Juanita rolled her eyes at his show of concern. "I'm alright."

"Love, come over and I will explain things to you. If you want to know, that is."

"Honestly, I'm not interested in your side of the story. It's too late for that."

"Fine. Just come then. We are still family."

Juanita dozed on the chair she had been sitting on, at the park. As her head began to fall again, she jerked up, to look if she was being watched. A little boy seating with his mum, who was openly breastfeeding her baby in the next seat to her, giggled at her...covering his mouth with his little hands. Juanita tried to smile at him, then began to doze again...

"Wake up!"

She jerked her head up, to find a man wearing the normal green overall uniform of the Agofure workers and drivers, scowling at her.

"I'm sorry." Juanita rubbed her eyes. "Is my bus ready? Have they called the passengers on my bus?" She got up, dragging her bag with her. "I'm sorry, I'm just so tired and weak. I hope I haven't caused any inconveniences or delay...?"

The man kept frowning at her. "I'm sorry, but you cannot travel with us. Go back to the counter with your ticket and your money will be refunded."

"What?" Oh, not another problem. It's like some forces were trying their best to stop her from leaving Delta. Oh, but they won't succeed.

"You mean, you replaced me already? But that's not fair..." She appealed to other passengers who were staring at her. Why were they looking at her with mouths opened? They should be supporting her against this injustice.

"I was only asleep for a couple of seconds and you've replaced me? Where's the bus? Where's the driver? I demand to see the manager!"

"I am the driver, and that is the bus." He pointed. Juanita hurriedly dragged her bag to the bus, but the passengers who were about to enter began to give way for her. The boy who was about to call the numbers on the tickets for the passengers to go in blocked her path.

"Where you dey go?" He asked, with a panicky expression.

Juanita turned on the driver, in frustration. "Why can't I go in? The bus hasn't even been loaded. Look..." She showed him her ticket. "This is my bus. Why can't I go in, why?

"Because..." He began smugly. "...you are mad."

Juanita was so angry, she slapped him, but he didn't even flinch. "How dare you call me mad? Is that how you treat your customers here? What impudence! Do I look mad? In fact, you're crazy, for calling me mad." She turned around to get clarification from the crowd that was building up.

"Good people, please do I look mad to you?" She appealed to their stunned faces.

"A crazy man can be recognized not by his words, but by his actions." He laughed at her, even as she lunged for his neck.

"Madam."

Juanita turned to see a fat bald man with a stern look on his face. " Er…yes?"

"Who are you talking to?"

What kind of question was that? She started to point at the driver, but he wasn't there! Jesus, what was happening to her? No wonder all these people were gathered. They all thought she was mad!

"Step away from the bus, please."

"Listen" She spoke calmly. "I'm not mad. He was here. He woke me up…"

"Madam, can you step away, please." His voice was sterner. "Abigail! Bring her money."

What? This was not happening. She looked at the counter-girl, hurrying out to get to the manager, then she saw the driver in his outfit, standing by the counter, with a clipboard in hand, about to sign a paper but he was too dazed from staring at her to sign.
"That's him!" Juanita shouted.

The driver stumbled backwards causing the clipboard and pen to fall. "Me, what?" He asked in fear. "I drink the blood of Jesus. Odi ebo sekewe." He snapped his finger at her, saying evil charms won't work.

"Was it not you that woke me up just now?" She started toward him. "How did you suddenly get there, away from me?"

"Hah!" The driver started to move away. "Make una stop this Ekpa from nearing me o." He said in broken English (Ekpa meaning mad). "I get wife and pikin for house o, I no won die ehhh."

People started to laugh, some just shook their head in pity.

"Such a pretty lady. People are wicked." A fat elderly woman in George clothing said bitterly.

"I'm not mad!" She cried in frustration as she swivelled at the thickening crowd. Then she saw him. He was standing at the back of the crowd, with his arms folded, sneering at her. "That's him! He's the one trying to make me look mad."

The crowd looked about, at themselves, but they didn't see him. Oh, she had to catch him to prove her sanity! She took off into the crowd and they gave way for the madwoman who ran out of the park shouting "Stop!"

The crowd followed and watched as the madwoman ran into the main road and was knocked down by a bike rider.

*　　*　　*　　*　　*

Juanita opened her eyes. Concerned honey eyes stared down at her, then the mouth smiled and called in a deep drawling voice.

"Mama, she's awake."

Juanita's eyes focused on the frail old woman who shuffled to her side. "Omome." Tears streamed down her eyes.

"Nana?" Juanita's confused gaze focused on the man. "Pastor?"

He chuckled. "It's Tega. The villagers just nicknamed me Pastor."

She tried to sit up, but couldn't. Then with apprehension, she realized she was bound. Hands tied apart with thick blue ropes and her legs bound together. Juanita closed her eyes as she had flashbacks. The last thing she remembered was trying to catch that man nobody else could see but her, and being knocked down by that bike man. She must have fainted or something. They had all thought she was crazy…she closed her eyes, as she remembered with a sickening feeling.

"Untie me." She growled.

"I don't think we should…" Nana began.

"Now!" Her eyes flew open with unshed tears.

Tega touched Nana's shoulder. "It's okay. She's fine –for now." Juanita did not miss the meaning of that statement, she hoped their assumptions that she was abnormal, was wrong. As Tega set her loose, she looked at him properly. He wasn't wearing dirty clothes today. He was on blue old jeans and a white T. shirt that showed off his biceps. Not bad at all. She raised her eyes to his face. He had that amusing smile again, as he stared back at her. She turned away.

"So…" She massaged her wrists. "How did I get back here?" She glanced about her mother's room in Kokori.

"Mama sent me to get you," Tega said.

"Your father called me," Nana said, as she sat on the bed. "He said he had been called on your handset and informed you were in the hospital."

34

"Okay…" Juanita sensed her grandma's hesitation to continue. "And that's why I was brought back to the village you told me never to come back to, and it's why I was bound too?" Nana looked away.

"You were in a terrible state," Tega supplied, resting against the wall. "I arrived on the same day of your accident. You had been sedated, because, according to the doctor, you've been paranoid, mumbling gibberish. The next morning you woke up at the hospital with a piercing scream."

Juanita watched calmly as Tega shuddered on his recount of what he had seen.

"When I rushed into the room, you had just lifted your bed and flung it against the window and you kept yelling for someone to leave you alone. I tried to hold you, but you were too strong, and you scratched my face." He pointed to a faint scar near his jaw. "I had some help from the hospital attendants and we tied you up. The doctor demanded you be transferred to a loony house, but Nana said to bring you back. And I totally agreed with her. You've been hysteric for five days straight. Today is a miracle." He finished, with a serious look on his face.

Tears streamed down her eyes. "And you brought me here… why? To die? Do you realize the city can treat better? You do realize this village killed my mother?

Tega handed her a handkerchief. "The village didn't kill her, her family did." Tega received a deadly look from Nana and raised his hands up. "I meant the other family."

"They are not her family." Nana spat out.

Juanita massaged her forehead. "Maybe it's time you tell me what's going on, Nana. Because I've tried to overlook it and just be gone. But whoever these other family are, they aren't letting me."

Nana sighed. "My child, it's a long story."

Juanita cackled. "Does it look like I'm going anywhere?"

Nana sighed again, then began the story.

"Our people used to say, a maiden who performs the maiden dance at the market square should not moan when the evil prince chooses her as his bride. Many years ago, when I was a young married woman, I was childless and my prominent husband, who is late now, married four wives, including me. All of them dropped babies like overripe fruits from a full tree…except me. Seven years straight, I had been prayed for, by the Igbe priestess, but I was still childless. These prayers only occurred once a year in April when the white witches came out in a full display of power, to heal, deliver and catch witches. As a child and follower of Igbe, you could always go to the river to pray on your own, with your basin and other items. You could even pray at home, and the goddess will hear you, as long as you performed the normal ritual. But it was strongly believed that if the priestess who had direct access to the goddess herself, on the day of the festival where all the messengers of the goddess are at attention to minister to us specially prayed for you, you would receive a speedy answer. But I was impatient. I was tired of dancing to the tune of the regular Igbes. I was enticed by the evil priestess of Igugu Igbe. Folklore has it that Igugu broke out from Agege Igbe. They were rebels and were not to be associated with. In fact, they held a different festival on December 24th. I danced to that tune and I got what I wanted.

Only, I not only married my offspring off to the god of the river, Ndichie, but I also brought the sanction of the evil Igugu Igbe goddess upon them."

Nana shook, as tears poured uncontrollably down her eyes. "It didn't occur to me then, how deep the covenant was. Any offspring of Igugu Igbe must continuously serve and pay homage to the goddess…must stay married to the spirit husband, Ndichie, who comes and make love to them at night." Juanita cringed.

"Some children have ignorantly gotten married to other men…" Nana continued. "But, it never last, and even when it does, they never have peace of mind. For example, your father; He impregnated your mother at an early age and even though he married her, still left for no just cause." She sighed. "If for any reason, these children rebel and serve another, denouncing them, the sanction will be evoked."

"And-" Juanita fidgeted. "What is this sanction?"

Nana looked at her with tears in her eyes.

"You will go mad until you eventually die." Juanita swallowed hard. She couldn't look at their faces. "Your mother" Nana continued, "…used to serve when she was small. But when she grew up and moved to the city, she became a Christian and forgot all about it. I became a Christian too, here in the village and just put it all behind me. Until she returned here in April, complaining about her life. She had said the only good thing going on for her, was her business and she had been having dreams that her problems came from here. I told her about our history and she made me follow her to the shrine of Igugu Igbe, where she renewed her vows, received powder from the priestess and returned to Lagos to serve God."

Tega snickered.

"Don't do that young man." She scolded him. "You don't understand these things."

"Why become a Christian then? Why not just serve them?" Juanita asked in frustration.

"Hah! Their demand is high, and me I want to go to heaven o. My pastor said you will go to hell if you served any other god. The bible says so."

"True," Tega agreed.

Juanita shook her head. "So, God has the power to help us make heaven, but no power to deliver us from Igbe?"

Nana frowned. "I didn't say that."

"What then, are you saying?" Juanita threw her hands up. "Your pastor was around, yet my mother died. Why didn't you take her to the shrine?"

"They rejected her."

"What?"

Nana fidgeted. "They wanted human blood."

"What?!" Juanita and Tega both exclaimed.

Juanita began pacing the room. She had a slight limp from the accident. This couldn't be happening. She thought. She never should have come down to this place. This was too much. Her steady life in the States, shattered by this backward illiterate village. They've been on the story for three hours straight and Nana wasn't finished yet.

"When the priestess poured the libation into the river, she had stated it was the blood of a maiden. She said it provoked the gods to answer speedily, compared to the blood of a cock, which was the normal method of Agege Igbe. When I begged them to save your mother, they demanded another maiden's blood. They said if your mother had not turned her back on them, it wouldn't have been necessary. But then, they had to appease the gods with pure blood, and I had to get it myself! I was a Christian!" Nana cried out. "Where and how, would I kill an innocent young girl? When that witch performed the ritual for me, many years ago. She got the blood herself!"

"Mama, calm down." Tega went and held her shoulders, but she shook him off.

"Don't worry my child," She spoke confidently to Juanita. "The true Igbe priestess has promised to help us. I will take you to her and everything will be okay, again."

"No, it won't!" Tega slapped the wall. "Don't you see...you are making the same mistake her mother made, by returning to them. Igugu and Agege are one Igbe. Whether one uses the blood of a cock or a maiden...they all still serve the devil. They are all married to Ndichie."

"Shut up!" Nana snapped. "What do you know? Because you go about preaching and helping people in the village doesn't mean you understand the deep sacred things."

"But I understand the deep secrets of God, by revelation through the Holy Spirit."

Juanita collapsed on the brown sofa and examined her bandaged right leg, totally ignoring them.

"There is no other way!"

"Jesus is the way!" Tega paused to catch his breath. "God can set her free. She doesn't have to conform to their will. What is the essence of claiming Christianity when you do not even believe He can save your grandchild?"

"The pastors do not understand these things." Nana shook her head regrettably. Believe me, son, I have tried the praying and fasting and binding. Pastor Osare did that. But my daughter still died. I will not let that happen to my last hope." She looked at Juanita, and their gaze locked. "You must water the thorn, for the sake of the rose."

CHAPTER EIGHT

Dec. 19th

The cock crowed raucously, as the priestess picked it and rolled it over Juanita's head. She was kneeling by the bank of the river and couldn't believe she was actually going through with it. She, a learned professional and practising lawyer, was in the village tying only a white wrapper and performing some ritual to some god. Thank God there were no pictures because she'd have died if this was posted on social media. The priestess broke the neck of the cock and flung it into the river.

"Agege Igbe. A man's work is from sun to sun, but a mother's work is never done. Your children are here again. Emo we na!" She cried out in Urhobo, praising and hailing the goddess. She poured powder all over Juanita's head and neck, shouting off more incantations, in tongues unknown to men. She sat Juanita on the little stool and told her to wash her hands in the basin. She placed the mirror in front of her and told her to repeat after her. "I Juanita, daughter to Ovore, daughter to the goddess, Igbe, pledge allegiance to you, oh great one and ruler of all waters, to serve and worship you for the rest of my life… ise." Juanita saw her reflection in the mirror tying only a white wrapper, with hair unbelievably long and powdered neck…smiling smugly at her. She gasped and dropped the mirror, but the priestess caught it.

"You fool" She scolded. "If this breaks, you die." She turned to Nana who had been watching the procedure apprehensively. "It is over now. She will not run mad, for she has renewed her covenant with the only true god. Make sure she travels with her basin, mirror and stool."

Juanita grimaced at the idea.

"Do not look for me anymore." The priestess allowed her male attendant who had been beating a single drum, during the ritual procession, to take her hand and support her weight, as he hung his drum behind him, with a cloth, serving as a rope.
"I am too old for this" She continued "…and I have to pass on to the world beyond. My

daughter will take over." Juanita and Nana thanked her and watched as they slowly left. Then Nana turned to her with a relieved smile on her face.

"It is over, dear."

"I think so," Juanita said, hopefully.

"Now, you must travel before our enemies find out what we have done. I don't think they can touch you, now that the goddess herself is protecting you, but we can never be too careful."

Juanita nodded wisely and they both left, carrying her new acquisitions. How was she supposed to travel with all these? She wondered.

That night, she slept peacefully without nightmares. It was truly over, Juanita thought as she prepared to leave the next morning. Thank God she listened to Nana. Her legs were a bit stiff, so she decided to go for a walk. After dressing in black tights, yellow singlet and black canvas, she started to walk down the street, but her bandaged leg began to hurt, and the more she walked, the more it hurt. So she turned and headed for the house. The pain was unbearable, her heartbeat began to speed up like she had been running. Her eyes began to spin. She wasn't going to collapse on the ground, was she? She wondered. It was barely past six in the morning, and there wasn't a soul on the dew-ridden street. It took all of her strength to get back into the compound.

"Nana!" She screamed, barely able to see the front door, as she stumbled against a stone and fell. Juanita's eyes rolled back into its sockets, she couldn't see. Nana rushed as fast as her weak legs could carry her, to her side. Juanita struggled to breathe, her eyes began to return to normal, she saw Nana's leg, so she grabbed it.

"Omome!" She could hear Nana saying …"You will not die!"
Juanita closed her eyes, even as she felt her breath leave her.

"Are you dead?"

Juanita's eyes flew open, at the sound of Nana's sneering voice. But that wasn't the biggest shock, the shocker was Tega strangling her neck, trying to kill her. She fought him with all her strength, managing to free a hand from her neck and biting it. Tega howled in pain and backed off.

"You witch!" Nana shouted angrily at her. "Why don't you just go ahead and die? Your mother never gave us this much trouble."

Juanita stared confused at the two of them. "Y –you two are in this together? Y –you are responsible for all that's been happening?"

"Yes!" They both chorused. Nana staring in fury at her and Tega sucking the finger she had bitten.

"B –but why?"

"Why?" Nana laughed hysterically. "What do you think? Igbe worshippers don't live long unless they were serving a particular purpose, and once it's achieved, they're called back to the underworld, to be sent again as a newborn child for another foolish woman seeking a baby! I am almost 100, and all shrivelled. I took your mother's blood to buy myself some time. You are so useless to me. We have no bond, why don't I just take your blood too, so I can last over a hundred years?"

Juanita shrieked with an animalistic cry and rushed for her grandma's face, scratching and pinching her.

"Kweke Kweke! Wa jere o!" Nana shouted for help, as she tried to hide from Juanita's nails. Tega shoved her off and stood between the two women.

"And you!" Juanita pointed her bloody fingers at him. "Why did you support this?"

"Because he wants your soul."

Juanita turned sharply to see Craig rushing in, from the green gate, panting, like he had been running. "Get away from them, Juan!"

Juanita frowned. "Craig? I thought you'd be in America by now?"

"I never left. I was with your father."

Juanita's head began to pound, so she held it with both hands. "What do you mean by he wants my soul?"

"Because he is in love with you. He has always been."

Juanita turned to look at Tega, he was holding Nana who had slumped to the floor. He looked up at her with scary eyes, then back at Nana's bleeding face.

"Juan baby, I know you don't understand that. But he's known you for a long time now and I'll explain it all to you later." Craig approached her slowly.
"Baby, I'm so sorry for leaving you. I was just sacred. But when I found out the whole truth, I couldn't let them kill you. Come on, take my hand and let's get out of here."

Juanita massaged her throbbing forehead. "This is so confusing. How can he take my soul? It does not make sense"

"These people are sick illiterates. Come!" He stretched his hand out impatiently. "I have a boat by the river. Now! Let's go!"

The river. Her mother. Juanita gasped for air and collapsed on the floor. She could hear a faint voice in her head saying… "Lose her and let her go, in the name of Jesus." So she began to say it too.

"Lose me and let me go, in the name of Jesus." She chanted quietly.

"Fight them, Juanita!" She could hear Tega's voice now. "Lose her and let her go, in the name of Jesus!"

She opened her eyes to see Tega praying over her. She could see a man rushing Nana out of the compound.

"Water" Her dry throat croaked.

"Bring me water!" She heard Tega shout out. To who? She wondered…before she passed out.

"Up Nepa!" Juanita could hear the children of the village shouting excitedly, so she turned her head to see that the light bulb in her mother's porch had come on. The light had been repaired after all. Tega stepped out of the house and sat beside her on the pavement, at the foot of the porch, passing her boiled groundnut in a bowl. She took it and cracked the shell loudly as she thought of Nana at the health centre. She had put her there, with her nails. She had scratched the old woman's face bloody, yesterday. Tears threatened to trickle down her cheeks.

"Where is your Americana?" Tega abruptly asked, jolting her back to the present.

Juanita chuckled. "Picked to his heels. Couldn't blame him for running from a madwoman."

"You are not mad." He said vehemently.

She turned to look at his stubborn set jaw with the scar, still visible, and then she remembered.

"Are you in love with me?"

Tega choked on a nut, he had thrown into his mouth and started coughing. Juanita just ignored him and waited for his reply.

"Where did that come from?" His eyes were a bit red and teary. "Who told you that?"

"Are you?" She looked him in the eye.

"Um, well…" He looked at his leather brown sandals and started to pick dirt from his toenails. "I wouldn't say 'love' per say."

"What would you say?"

Tega sighed and looked at her with that half-smile, only now, he looked shy. "The thing is I've had a crush on you since I was ten. I know it's crazy…" He quickly added as he saw her expression. "…I tried to get out of the ridiculous situation but I couldn't…especially since you returned to the country."

Juanita's frown deepened. "But I never knew you until recently."

"Wrong. We used to play together in your parent's house at Lagos."

Juanita's face lighted up. "Tegus, the village boy?"

Tega rolled his eyes. "God! Of all the things to remember. I speak well now, you know?"

Juanita laughed. "Your mum was our house help and she lived in our boys quarter with you and your sisters!"

"Yes. And before you ask, my sisters are married and living in Lagos, the younger one lives in Warri main town. My mom's been ill and that's why I'm here in the village, to take care of her."

"Oh."

"Yes."

"So…" Juanita eyed him. "You had a crush on me?"

"Still do." His honey eyes stared back at her, and she watched as his gaze stopped at her lips.

Juanita cleared her throat and Tega jolted back upright.

"Em," he stood up. "So! What do you intend to do?"

Juanita drew on the ground with her finger. "Let's see. What are my options? I tried to escape – no way. Tried to serve them –no way, so…ah, the option left –run mad and die."

Tega squatted in front of her and held her shoulders. "You don't have to. There is one option left."

"And what's that?" She asked, resignedly.

"Fight."

CHAPTER NINE

"With the children of God, the devil never wins, unless you don't fight," Tega said. "You've tried to run, but it didn't work, you even tried to appease them, still they want your life. You haven't shown them how powerful you are."

"But that's it, Tega!" Juanita bolted up, creating a gap between them. "I don't have any power. Hell! I don't even have a gun to just shoot them dead, that's if it will work, considering the fact that I'm dealing with spirit beings."

"For we wrestle not against flesh and blood, but against principalities and powers, rulers of wickedness in high places..." Tega turned her to him, "...but all power has been given unto you, to tread upon serpents and scorpions and no harm shall come near you..."

Juanita smiled wistfully. "You certainly know your bible well. Now I see why the villagers call you 'Pastor'. But what good is it when Nana's pastor couldn't save my mom –and you are not even a real pastor."

"It is true what your Nana said..." Tega held her cheeks. "...that these pastors do not understand. For it is written, my people perish for lack of wisdom. It takes understanding Ani, and I understand. I can help you."

"Okay..." Juanita nodded thoughtfully. "How do we fight, then? Do you know where to buy a gun?" She asked at an attempt to humour. "Or do you have dynamites so we can blow their shrines to blazes. You know where the wicked Igbe shrine is, don't you?"

He narrowed his eyes at her and the corner of his mouth turned up in a half-smile. Juanita loved it when he did that...Focus! She cautioned her herself.

He stepped back, dipping both hands into the back pockets of his jean. "You have to give your life to Christ."

"I'm a Christian."

"Yeah, sure." He smirked.

"No, seriously."

"Really?" Juanita laughed at his sceptical look.

"Fine. I used to go to church. But in America, I never had time for it."

"You need Him, Ani. There's no other way but Him."

She sighed. "Okay. I can do that."

"You have to be serious."

"I am serious!" She snapped. "Can't you see that? I'd bump into a beehive if it would set me free!"

"Oh, you are serious. Okay…" He began to pace. "First of all, you will confess Jesus as your Lord, you'll bring repentance on behalf of yourself and family, for all the worshipping of idols, deities, Igbe, and the like. Next, you will renounce and divorce all Igbe and water spirits, by the prayer points I will lead you through. Then we can disconnect and pull down their stronghold over your life."

Juanita waited for him to continue, but he just lifted an eyebrow at her. "That's it?" She chuckled. "My mother died because she didn't do all these?"

"I can't answer that, Ani. But I do know that casting and binding without knowing or getting to the root of the issue, will be a total waste of time on the part of the pastor. That reminds me, we are fasting tomorrow. We will do battle tomorrow."

Juanita turned up her nose. 'Can't you fast for me or something?"

"Remember, you'd bump into a beehive to set yourself free?" She looked at her slippers-clad feet. "Jesus told his disciples…about the demon-possessed man…this kind cannot go out, except by prayer and fasting."

"I am not possessed."

He held her hand. "Come on, let's go see your grandma."

When Juanita saw her grandma's face, she burst into tears. Her entire face was swathed in bandages, and the only visible thing was her eyes, nose and patched lips. Nana, upon hearing her, beckoned for them to come forward. Tega held Juanita in his arms, as they shuffled to her side. They sat at the foot of the bed, even as a nurse propped Nana up on the pillow.

"Omome," Nana began, "don't cry. It is not your fault." Her tiny voice sounded hoarse. "The goat thought it was dirtying its owner's wall till it realized its coat was peeling. I brought this upon us all. We can't defeat them. We tried to be smart, now look… they own us, they know how to deal with us." Nana joined Juanita in wailing.

Tega sighed, as he pondered leaving Juanita's side, to console Nana. He chose to stay put. "Nana, Ani, you two need to stop. It's not over yet. There is hope. Ani, tell her we have plans…"

Nana shook her head. "There isn't, my son. Believe me." Her cataract filled eyes bore holes into them. "I remember my mother told me I was born years ago, on the day of our yam festival, that makes me almost a hundred years old. There is nothing that these eyes have not seen under the sun. Let me tell you something you don't know…" The nurse left the room, and Nana waited for her to close the door before she continued.

"I was a beautiful woman in my maiden days. The town called me Erhuwu…beauty…for I was among the fairest. But I was cursed by those envious of me. I was married for twelve years without an issue, I had to go back to my father's house. Then this wealthy Chief Okagbare who had two wives before me came into my life. I lost two babies in the womb, within seven years. My husband married another…I became a laughing stock, when she gave birth like a hen, scattering her chicks everywhere…" Nana lifted her eyes as she flashed back…

*   *   *   *   *

March 30th 1970

Emetetiabo sobbed softly on her bamboo bed. She was alone in the little mud house that served as her private chambers. The raffia mat, which served as curtains to the door-less room, was parted and in came Chief Okagbare on only a wrapper, tied scantily around his waist. He frowned as he observed her. He removed his chewing stick from his mouth and spat on the bare ground, Emetetiabo hid her disgust as she knelt down.

"Osare me, miguo." She greeted in Urhobo, saying my husband, welcome.

"Vre-doh." He licked his teeth, as he gestured for her to rise. "I came to lie with my pretty wife," He continued in their native dialect. "…but it seems your woes have clouded you –again. What ails you this time?"

"Osare me, my husband," She repeated. "Is there an end to my woes? Is there an end to what ails me? Have my fellow wives and the villagers stopped laughing at me? Leave me, let me weep, for the gods have cursed me to be childless. It's the cross I must bear."

"Woman, stop talking rubbish." He said, irritably. "The gods did not curse you."

She turned on him. "Your young wife, Ikebe, she called me a witch, that I have eaten all my children in the spirit world. Me! I had a dream about her before I woke up with tears. She is the witch. She took my Banga, that I had set aside to prepare soup, and replaced it with her spoilt ones. My mother arrived and showed her pepper, digging her nails into her ugly face!"

"Enough!" Chief turned. "I will go seek who is ready for me."

"You mean Ikebe right?" She began to cry. "Oh my husband, Is this how I shall perish?"

He sighed exasperated and looked at her. "Your father has always taken you to the priestess for blessings. Yet, no result. I am fed up with your childless state too. I say you go to Orhurhu…"

Emete gasped. "Orhurhu, the priestess of Igugu Igbe? She's evil!"

"Fine. Don't go."

"My father is taking me tomorrow to see the priestess before the general festival."

Chief smirked. "Let your father be ready to marry you if you don't eventually have a child." With that, he left her room, and the tempo of her wailings, increased.

* * * * *

Nana shook her head bitterly at the both of them. "That was how I sold my soul to the devil. I visited Orhurhu, and on the very same day of Igbe festival, we went to the river, where she prayed for me. I took in that night, after laying with my husband, but I had a dream…" Nana recounted the events of her dream…

Emetetiabo, as a young wife, wearing one of her brown expensive wrappers, tied tightly under her armpit, walked gracefully towards the river, with an earthen pot on top her head. As soon as two female children spotted her, they stood up from the ground, where they had been waiting.

"Ive" The bigger one of about twelve called to the little one of five. "I have found the one I was waiting for, you must go back to mother now."

Emete paused to observe them. "Nooo" cried Ive. "We must go back together or I follow you."

"Don't be naughty! What will mother say? My mission is to follow this woman, yours is to go back to mother."

Emete's pupils widened as understanding dawned on her. These were spirit children. But why does that one want to follow her?

"But Khire, we just got reunited not long ago, and you want to leave me again?"

Khire smiled and pat her sister's head. "I always return, don't I? I won't be long now. This woman has requested for me and I must serve mother…"

"Enh!" Emetetiabo began to walk hurriedly away from the river. "Echaibo! Go back to your spirit mother. I don't want you for a child." But Khire kept following her and shouting back to sad Ive… "I shall return!"

"I woke up knowing that I had been given a child who was bound to return to the spirit world," Nana said.

My husband and I could not find Orhurhu, she would not see us. So we visited other priestesses. They all assured us, after a series of sacrifices, that she wasn't' going anywhere. That she was going to remain in the land of the living. Little did I know that Igugu Igbe was laughing at my naivety."

"Do you know what your mother told me?" Nana stared at Juanita. "When she was brought to the village after the sanction had started? She wasn't herself that fateful evening, she looked at me and smiled, saying she was sorry, that she had to go. She said her people were calling her a thief and a deserter, who had been sent on an assignment and refused to return from the land of the living."

Juanita massaged her temples. "So, all these while, they had every intension of taking her back."

"Just as they intend to take you too." Tega said quietly.

"God forbid!" Nana coughed out. Juanita just buried her face in her palms and sobbed, even as Tega embraced her.

CHAPTER TEN

Juanita was sprawled on the floor of Tega's living room, face-up, with her black T.shirt pulled up, exposing her flat tummy. She kept looking at the wall clock, whose hand read 15min past 6. Tega walked in from his room and paused at seeing her.

"You look like a displaced person in a refugee camp."

"I'm sure I feel worse than them. This is an inhuman subjection!"

Tega laughed. "It's called fasting...and you need to stop looking at the clock." He added, as her eyes wandered to the clock again. "Get up, go home, pray and freshen up, before you know what's happening, it will be passed 8. Then you can break your fast."

"But we've been praying all day!"

Tega went to her, and pulled her reluctant form, up.

"Can't I just stay here? That house scares the shit out of me." She embraced him and refused to let go.

Tega closed his eyes, as a whiff of her scent assaulted his nose. He shook his head mentally. "Your grandma needs you, now that she isn't quite well. We'll see tomorrow, Ok?"

Juanita pulled away. "Why? To continue the Fast? Fine. Let's hope you don't come to carry my corpse by morning." She picked up her handbag from a blue plastic chair and walked towards the door.

He chuckled at her unsteady walk. "More like I'll be carrying a bag of bones."

"Haha." She gave a fake laugh and stepped outside. "Don't escort me." She jammed the door in his face. Tega put his head against the door and smiled. But a knock jolted him a few seconds later.

"Can't stay away from me, much?" His smile was wiped off as he opened the door and saw Ikebe smiling sheepishly at him.

"My pastor, my pastor."

She cat-walked into his living room, wearing her best brown wedge-sandals, with a faded black mini skirt and a yellow blouse tied under her burst, exposing her pot-belly. She smacked her chewing gum as she looked about the small room, with one long red couch and a white one for two, plus a centre table made from oak, with a bible and a bottle of water on it. His carpet was checkered with white and black, the white fan hanging from the ceiling matched the colour of his walls. It was a neat room. Ikebe frowned.

" I come to help clean your house o."

Tega sighed. "Ikebe, as you can see, it is clean. Thanks, though."

"Yes." She looked around again, not quite satisfied. Then, she smiled sheepishly. "How is you?"

"It's... 'How ARE you'... And I'm fine."

Ikebe rolled her eyes as she moved closer to him and pressed her chest against his frame.

"Na why I like you. You dey speak correct English, you kon fine sef. You na still city person. I want make you marry me. You no go ever hungry again. I go dey cook better better soup for you."

"Ikebe..." He tried to remove himself from her embrace, but her grip was strong. "...I'm not hungry. And I'm interested in someone else. Don't worry, your own will come."

"Who be that person? See enh, pastor, if no be you, I go die o, I go kill myself for your house! As I dey talk now sef, konji don dey hold me. Come see me perform for bed." She started dragging him to the bedroom. "Or you won do am for here?"

"That's it." He grabbed her upper arms and shoved her towards the main door. "I'm not sleeping with you. Stop your madness at once!" He shoved her out and turned the key. Then, he went to his room, ignoring her incessant banging on his door.

The following day, Tega sat on the porch of Juanita's house, lifting his bible and anointed oil in a plastic bottle, getting ready to leave. Juanita came out of the house.

"You're leaving already? Won't you eat, first? I thought after those hours spent praying, we were done for today."

Tega looked sceptically at the plate she proffered. It was bread and sardine. "That won't even last me on my 15mins journey to my house."

She rolled her eyes. "Don't mock me, cause I can't cook our native food. Nana is still on bed rest and I'm famished as hell."

"I'll eat at home. My mom must have prepared something."

"Your mom…" Jaunita began eating the sandwich. "I still haven't seen her, you know?"

"The other time you came, she was at their market women meeting. You want to come see her?"

She thought about this for a few seconds. "Actually, I wanted you to take me to this famous river."

Tega stared at her. "Are you sure?"

"Positive."

He shrugged. "Fine. I might as well eat your pitiful meal." He laughed as she tried without success, to keep him away from the bread.

*   *   *   *   *

"So, what do you do?" Juanita asked as they strolled through the lonely narrow path, leading to the river.

"I'm a trader. I own two shops. An electronic and provision store."

"You shut them down, to come and take care of your mum?"

"Well, I have a sales boy in each store." Tega kicked a pebble against a tree, causing it to rattle and birds shrieking, flew out.

"Trustworthy?"

He shrugged. "I think. I hope. These Igbo boys are truly something. But I do bookkeeping. They are to give me proper details of all their sales when I return."

"Is it lucrative?"

"Well, I calculate my profit, quarterly. And I earn, close to a million naira in those three months."

"Hmmm"

He chuckled. "What? Not good enough for your rich classy standard?"

She snickered. "Not bad for a village boy." Tega shoved her playfully, even as they reached the river. She stopped laughing as she looked at the still waters, occasionally disturbed by two young boys splashing in it. "Is this it? I thought it would be formidable or something."

It was his turn to snicker. "Like you'd see the goddess taking a bath at the centre, looking all beautiful but scary?"

She rolled her eyes at his sarcasm. "Yea, something like that."

"Well, no. It's just like the other river we have in the village. It's normal...except for when someone mysteriously disappears. The villagers would rather use Oke river for their laundry, cooking and bathing. It's safer. Here, only the bold come here...and of course, fearless children. Others mostly come here to pray and offer sacrifices."

"Hmmm..." They both turn at the sounds of feet running towards them. Two men stopped in front of them, panting.

"Ogho, what is it?" Tega asked the shorter man.

"Your house, your house..." He was breathless.

"E dey burn!" The other one shouted.

"My mother!" Tega exclaimed and began to run home, with the others tagging along.

He could see smoke rising from his room window. People were gathered shouting and watching. Some men had mixed soapy water and were trying to quench the fire, from the kitchen's back door. The kitchen was ablaze. Then he saw his mother, with Ikebe holding her as she explained what had happened. Tega was headed towards her, but he suddenly stopped and looked at the house. His room was next to the kitchen. Juanita saw the look in his eyes and began to run towards him.

"Tega, no!" She screamed. But he was already staggering towards the back door.

"My documents…my certificate…they are all in there." He mumbled as he got to the door.

Juanita got to him, and pulled him with all her might, causing him to fall on top her, even as the door exploded, and flew a few feet away from them, causing people to scream and step back.

"My pikin!" His mother hurried to where they had fallen. "I don't know what happened …" She began to narrate in Urhobo.
"I was in my room…" She continued in their native dialect. "…when I heard something explode in the kitchen. I went in, to see that it was on fire. Maybe is the new gas cylinder you brought. If we were using our stove, this would not have happened."

"My documents are gone!" Tega shouted as he shrugged off Juanita's hands. "This should not have happened!"

"Calm down. Look, the men have put out the fire." Juanita pointed. Tega hurried into the smoky house and straight to his room. Juanita followed him. A young man placed his arm on Ikebe's shoulder, stopping her from following them.

"Obruche, what?" She asked, irritably.

"My Bebe, which one be the English you dey form for me? Make we sha dey go house, we don try."

Ikebe jerked away from him. "You no see say Pastor need consolement? Abeg shift, make I see road." She shoved him off and went inside the house.

Another guy came and stood beside him. "I no tell you say na pastor she like? Wetin you won do now? Wetin be consolement sef?"

Obruche smiled mischievously. "You go soon know. Make we waka." They bounced their way out of the compound.

Tega held black pieces of papers, in his hands and bowed his head, as if to mourn them. "All my documents. I carried them down here because I thought it was safer. Why did I do that?"

Juanita put her hand on his shoulder. "Calm down."

"Stop telling me to calm down!" He flared, as he rose from the floor where he had squatted. "I had my B.sc certificate there. I was going to apply for a Masters programme in Business Administration. How do you think I'm going to do that now?"

Jaunita stepped back. "You sound like it was my fault."

"Isn't it? Can you explain this fire, which consumed the kitchen and my room? Don't you realize it's the powers we wrestle against that are after me now, for trying to help you?" He spat out angrily.

She stepped farther back and whispered, tears blurring her eyes. "It was an accident."

"It wasn't! It was a warning." He watched as she turned on her heel and ran out. But he didn't try to stop her. He just sat on the blackened floor and allowed Ikebe who had just come in, pat his back.

CHAPTER TEN

Juanita stood by the riverbank and stared beyond the water. There was no one there today. She was starving. It was the second day of not hearing from Tega. She had gone to his house and found men repairing the affected areas, but no sign of him. She had been fasting on her own, since yesterday and did the best she could do in the place of prayers. But today, was more like a hunger strike, than a fast. She wasn't in the mood to pray and it was already evening.

She suddenly had an urge to enter the water. She couldn't swim, she reminded herself, but she went in, anyway. When the water got to her knees, she thought to return, but the still waters came alive, pushing and urging her to go farther. She remembered her dream, of her mum being engulfed by the water. Maybe she should just drown, she thought to herself. What was she living for? Who was she living for? If the only person who had set out to help her, had absconded, then she had no hope left. She'd rather die than run mad on the streets. She went in farther. She could barely walk steadily. The current had become too strong. The water was at her breast now…

"Ani!"

She stopped moving. She knew that voice, and only one person called her that. Was this another nightmare? Won't they let her drown in their river too?

"Juanita, don't you dare move any farther!"

She swivelled to see Tega thrashing into the river, running and stumbling towards her. Her face lighted up. It was real, he was really here. She raised her right hand in greeting but abruptly slipped under the water. She tried to stand, but her injured leg suddenly decided to torment her with piercing pain. She tried to scream, but water rushed into her mouth and nose. She was going to die. This realization struck her and she fought even harder. She wanted to live. Strong hands grabbed her right hand, which was still outstretched, and dragged her to the surface.

Tega held her in both hands and thrashed back to the bank, as she gasped for air. They fell on a heap on the wet ground, crying.

"You're so stupid! What were you doing?" Tega cried out. "You could have killed yourself. Didn't I tell you the river was dangerous?"

"You left me." Her entire body trembled. "You left. Just like Craig." She wiped tears furiously from her cheeks. "I —I didn't know what to do. I wanted to just…"

"…Kill yourself? Is that it, Ani?" He sighed and held her trembling body to him, planting kisses all over her face. "Don't you ever do that again. You hear me?" She nodded. "I love you, Ani, so much, it hurts my chest. If you die, I die."

He kissed her again, on the lips, long and sensual. She said nothing, so he went for her neck, sliding her wet yellow singlet off her shoulders. His fingers caressed her bareback, even as the setting sun gleamed against her arms. She let out a tiny cry and he covered her parted lips with his, gunning for her tongue. This time, she kissed him back and clung to him, as if for her dear life. Juanita tore at his wet grey shirt, which was glued to his body, ripping all the buttons, then she returned the favour, touching and kissing him all over, but she couldn't get enough, so she pulled her singlet over her head and flung it to the side, exposing her black bra, and the heaving top of her breast. Tega grabbed both of her hands, and held them down, as he pushed her gently until she was laying on her back. He kissed the top of her breast, freed one hand and unclasped her bra. Then he placed the hand inside her bra and massaged her breast slowly. Juanita let out another cry. He was going to make her cum, by just touching her. She had never experienced anything like it. She grabbed his belt, with her free hand.

"Take me." She whispered fiercely. "Make love to me."

Tega didn't need to be told twice. He went for her navel, circling his tongue around it. Her moans were encouraging. The orange-red sun had a wonderful glow and reflection on the river. Birds were chipping lovingly. The wind blew softly. The weather was just perfect. The entire atmosphere seemed to give its consent, urging them on. Tega abruptly stopped, coming to his senses. Jesus. He shook his head physically as if to shake a powerful force from him.

"Jesus." He muttered. With shaky hands, he hooked her bra back and sat upright.

Confused, Juanita opened her eyes and sat up too. "Why did you stop?"

"We have to."

"What do you mean we have to? How can you get me in this state and leave me hanging? You have to finish what you started." She grabbed both cheeks and kissed him, but he pulled her hands gently off.

"Ani, please. It's what they want."

She looked hurt. "You just told me you love me."

"With all that is good in me."

"Then prove it!"

"I am trying!" He stood up and found her singlet. He stretched it out to her. "I don't want to defile you."

She laughed hysterically and grabbed her singlet from him. "What the fuck are you talking about defilement? Are you doing it without my consent or did I tell you I was a freaking virgin?"

Tega tried his best to tidy up his shirt. "He that breaks the hedge, the serpent will bite." He tried to hold her but she slapped his hand away. "Don't you see it's what they want? They want you to sin and get polluted, so they can attack you again. We are winning Ani, and they are getting desperate. That's why they attacked me. And I didn't run, I actually went to drop my mum at Warri, with my sister, where she would be safe. I could never leave you to bear this alone." He took her hand, but she shoved him hard.

"Don't you ever touch me again, you piece of shit!" She ran off, struggling to put on her singlet.

*　　*　　*　　*　　*

Ikebe whistled excitedly as she walked down the road, wearing a brown rumpled and short gown, carrying a black poly bag in her right hand.

"Where you think say you dey go?"

Ikebe jumped at the sound of the voice, only to hiss when she saw Obruche and his friend, Apko, sitting on the trunk of a fallen tree.

"Wetin concern you?" She retorted.

"Wetin you dey carry?" Apko pointed at her nylon.

"Wetin concern you?" She repeated.

"You dey go that man house, no be so?" Obruche stood up.

"That man is pastor."

"You dey follow am up and down abi? You won make I slap that mouth wey you dey take call am pastor? Ashawo like you."

She shifted backwards, as he came close to her. "I be ashawo, yet you dey find how you go take enter my thing. I and pastor like each other. Na for your clear eyes, we go take marry born fine fine children like my pastor."

Obruche clenched his fist. "Why you dey talk like this na? No be you I tell say I wan marry, no be im make me they buy you gifts wey you dey share with your foolish friend?"

Ikebe laughed. "How you think say correct babe like me, go marry okada driver like you? You dey dream! Abeg, clear road for me jor, I shall now go and meet my love. Nonsense people." She hissed and eyed them both before she walked off. Apko stood up and joined Obruche to watch her go. Both had a menacing look.

Tega unlocked and pushed his front door open. But as he entered and was about to close the door, Ikebe rushed in, breathing like she had been running.

"Ikebe, what is the matter?" Tega asked, alarmed.

She hugged him. "I see you from far, so I just run to catch you."

"Is that it?" He separated himself from her.

"Yels." She offered the poly bag. "I bring you food. Sweet Banga soup and Usi, with bush meat."

"Ikebe, I thought it was something serious." He eyed the bag sceptically, before collecting it. "Er, thank you."

"Ya welcome." She smiled sheepishly.

He rolled his eyes. "You know say you fit speak Urhobo or Pidgin English and I go understand?"

She pouted. "But I wan learn na. If we marry na, I no wan disgrace you. I must show say I be correct wife for you."

Tega sighed. "Ikebe, I'm not marrying you."

"Ha, pastor, na lie o. You don dey like me. Remain small, you go kon love me. After today, our love go strong..."

"What are you doing?" Tega watched, aghast, as she zipped her gown down.

She frowned as she noticed his opened, wrinkled shirt. "Wetin happen to you?" Then she looked at his rippling chest. "Chai, pastor, you fine o. Our pikins go fine well well."

"Stop, at once!" His firm words didn't stop her from sliding off her gown, standing in all her nakedness. His mouth fell open as he stared. Then he laughed, confusing Ikebe. "Devil, you are such a joker!"

She didn't understand him, so she just grabbed him and put her head against his chest, forcing her naked breast on him. "I wan make you give me belle. You must enter me today."

"Ikebe, let go." He struggled to push her off. "This is wrong, and it's a sin. God won't be happy with either one of us. It's fornication. Plus I'm fasting for something very important. Please, don't ruin it."

"Pastor, no be you say, the violent take am by force? Omo, na my thing be this o. I must take am by force. All those village girls and Oke, dem no fit thief my joy. Pastor, na me you must want." She pulled out his belt, with one move, and unzipped his black pants.

"Jesus." He held his trousers up. "Ikebe, you've been attending church. Behave like a child of God and he will bless you at the right time."

"This blessing must not pass me by!" She grabbed him by the balls.

"Shiiiiiiiiiiit!" Tega, realizing she wouldn't reason with him, grabbed her arms and twisted, but she was surprisingly strong, panting like a beast, she bent down and thrust his dick into her mouth. Tega howled and slapped her hard across the face, she stumbled to the floor but rushed at him again. Tega looked at her determined eyes, he knew he had to get out of there. As she came at him, with an animalistic cry, he shoved her so hard, her head bounced against the wall and she slumped to the floor. But Tega didn't wait to see if she got up, he just fled from his house, dragging his trouser with him. He didn't see Obruche and Apko watching him from a tree opposite his compound. They waited for him to run out of sight, then sauntered into his compound, looking suspiciously, left and right. They found Ikebe on the floor of the sitting room, still stark naked, holding her bleeding head. She saw them and tried to sit up.

"Na pastor, im rape me." She cried out. "Help me, before I die for here." She stretched out her bloody hand. Obruche's eyes narrowed at her, he exchanged a glance with Apko, who nodded, and they both advanced her.

CHAPTER ELEVEN

Tega slapped his ear, to stop the mosquito, singing unpleasantly, around it. He came into consciousness as he heard a faint noise. He opened his eyes, and the noise got louder. Where was he? He looked about, then he remembered. He had run from Ikebe yesterday and had slept in the market. Raising his head up, he saw a crowd of villagers facing him, but they were a few feet away, they were shouting at the two elderly men that stood in front of them, backing Tega. Then he spotted Juanita, making her way through the crowd. As he made to get up, a hand forced his head back down, confused, he looked up to see, Mama Tina, one of his mother's friend, using her basket filled with green leaves to block anyone's view of him.

"My pikin, if you no one die today, no come out." She whispered and looked away.

Juanita wondered what all the fuss was about. The only reason she had joined was that she kept hearing 'die' and 'Pastor' and she knew that was Tega. She didn't understand as people kept on relaying the stories in Urhobo. She was anxious to know what had happened. Was he dead? The thought of it sent shivers down her spine.

"We go kill am!"

"Yes!" The youths shouted again at themselves, and at the elderly men.

"My children" One of the old men in front, called out. He was wearing an old white singlet with a wrapper wrapped around him and tied behind his neck. "...biko, calm down. Let us summon the young man first, so he can tell us what happened. After all, we all know he's a good boy. Most of you call him Pastor..."

The uproar was even louder. One youth rushed to the front and scraped his cutlass on the sand, causing dust to fly everywhere. "We no go gree!"

"Yes!" The crowd responded.

"Yes!" Obruche repeated. "Wetin we wan call am for? So he fit lie? No be me and Apko see am when he run commot for him house, with his trouser almost down?"

"Tufia!" A middle-aged woman spat on the ground.

"When we enter his house," Obruche continued. "We see Ikebe for the floor, dey bleed, naked!"

"Echaibo!" Another woman spat out.

"She tell us say Tega rape her anyhow, scatter her insides. She even show us him shirt wey she tear when them dey fight, but pastor overpower am. Before we fit take am go health centre, she die." Obruche raised Tega's torn grey shirt up.

Another uproar took over. Men shouted in anger. Women cried.

Goosebumps crept all over Juanita's arm. That was the same shirt Tega wore at the river, but she was the one who tore the buttons out, not Ikebe. What was going on? Could it be true? Could Tega have rejected her, who had given herself on a silver platter to go rape somebody else?

People began to clear the road, for the four men carrying Ikebe's corpse, covered in a white sheet. They dropped the baboon platform upon which she was placed, in front of the elders, who was beckoning on the crowd to calm down. The other elderly man called a midwife, who had been standing at the corner, arms akimbo, and she walked up smartly to the men. The three of them whispered for a few seconds, then she nodded and went to the corpse.
The people kept quiet as they watched her raise the sheet slightly and dipped two fingers into her vagina. When she extracted her fingers, she crumpled her face as she raised and showed everyone the tips which were covered with sperm.
"Man enter." She said, affirmatively.

The crowd went crazy. Oke, Ikebe's friend began to cry uncontrollably.

"Na food ooo." She threw herself on the ground. "Na food Ikebe go give Pastor because say him kitchen burn. She just dey do good girl ooo."

"Burn him house! Anywhere he run go, we go catch am." Apko shouted, and the crowd surged in anger in the direction of Tega's house.

*   *   *   *   *

Juanita couldn't watch his house burn anymore, she turned and started walking back home. She entered the house within fifteen minutes, still wondering where Tega was. He must know he was wanted, that's why he was hiding. Does this mean he is guilty? Tega? She shook her head physically. She went to Nana's room but found the frail woman asleep. So she closed the door and went to her mother's which she had been sleeping in. As she was closing the door, she jumped at the sight of Tega behind it.

"What are you doing here? They are combing the town, looking for you."

"Shhhhh" He looked outside, before closing the door behind her. "I was afraid, you might be followed."

"Why will anyone follow me?"

"Because they've been seeing us together. Oh, Juanita, this whole thing is just..." He tried to touch her, but she shrank back. He frowned. "You don't believe I did it do you?"

"She was found dead at your place. Naked. Where were you?"

"Dear Lord, I don't know what happened. She came to my place, yes, and she tried to force herself on me, I pushed her hard, but I didn't think it would kill her!"

58

Juanita was fuming. "Did she force your dick up her V? 'cause your sperm was found in her."

"Ani, I didn't rape her."

"But you had sex."

"What rubbish are you talking about? I can't believe you think I'd do such a thing!" He raked his short hair with his ten fingers. "Look, I can't stand here and wait for them to come get me." He stormed out of the house, but she didn't try to stop him. She just sat on the bed and massaged her temple. It wasn't up to two minutes when she heard a loud burst from the sitting-room door. Had Tega returned? As she stood up, her room door burst open, and Obruche leading two touts, rushed into her room, shoving her on the floor.

"Where him dey?" Obruche demanded, wielding his cutlass at her, while his fellows trashed the room as if looking for someone or something.

"W —what is going on?" Juanita asked, not daring to take her eyes off the cutlass, pointed at her.

"Where your fake boyfriend? Where Tega?" He shouted at her.

"What...why? Why would he be here?"

One of the touts angrily faced her. "You think say we no dey see una dey parade the village, together? You no wan bring am out? E dey the other room?" The three of them stormed out of the room.

"No! Nana is in there." She rushed after them, but they were already scattering the room, leaving a dazed Nana to gape at them, from her bed. They went back to the sitting room and turned it upside down too. Next, to the kitchen, then the backyard. With their energy spent, they returned to the sitting room, where Juanita was waiting for them.

"If you see am..." Obruche spat out. "Tell am say, men dey find am." His eyes roamed over her entire body, sending shivers down her spine.

Juanita swallowed. "Leave my house."

The third tout snared at her. "Your boy-boy rape, come kill our Ikebe, and your mouth dey sharp. Make we even rape you, sef."

Juanita stepped back. "Leave my house, now!"

Obruche laughed menacingly and led his gang out. Juanita waited for them to leave the compound, then she ran to the door and bolted it. She collapsed against it, holding her fast-beating chest. Nana came into the sitting room, leaning heavily on her stick. Juanita got up to go assist her. She raised the brown cushion from its overturned state and gently lowered Nana on it.

"This is all Tega's fault." She said angrily, as she began tidying the room. "I have enough problems as it is, already, without him having to add his. Only God knows what he did to that girl."

"Only God…?" Nana paused her lips. "What about you, Omome, don't you know?"

"Nana, you don't know what has been going on. The whole village is looking for Tega. They said he raped and killed one Ikebe girl."

Nana frowned and thought for a moment. Then she squinted at Juanita. "But, what do you say?"

"Nana, what does it matter what I say?" She sighed exasperatedly. "I wasn't there."

"And the villagers were?"

"Well…no."

"Do you truly believe he did it?" Juanita looked at her unclad feet. "Have you ever heard of Tega behaving like a hoodlum? Do you not understand why he is called a Pastor, even though he doesn't own or pastor a church?"

Juanita sighed. "I don't want to believe it."

"Then don't." Nana grabbed her hand, with surprising strength. "Can't you see it's a plot by our enemies? You have not been having nightmares for some days now. They are trying to destroy your helper because they know you are winning."

Juanita's eyes narrowed thoughtfully. "Tega said the same thing."

Nana pulled her down until their eyes levelled. "There is hope. They are shaken. Now is the time to fight back. Go, I won't stop you. Find him. Go!" She pushed Juanita, who stood up and rushed towards the entrance.

"Wait!"

"What?" She turned impatiently.

Nana giggled. "You do not have any shoes on." Juanita looked at her feet and began to shake with laughter until tears stained her cheeks.

CHAPTER THIRTEEN

Armed with a kitchen knife, stuck in her blue jean, and dressed in a black polo with black snickers, Juanita began her search for Tega. She was ready for the likes of Obruche. She went by his house, even though she knew she wouldn't find him there. The bungalow had been levelled to the foundation with fire. Not a single wall stood. She shook her head sadly at the debris, wondering what the poor man did to lose it all. He just wanted to help her. She looked up at the few people still gathered about, gossiping and staring at the ruins. A woman with a baby tied at her back, pointed at her, as she whispered in another woman's ear. Before Juanita knew what was going on, they were all staring at her. No one said anything anymore, they just stared. Goosebumps crept up her arms. She started to turn away, but she leaned too much on her bad ankle, and stumbled, gritting her teeth at the pain. As she walked away, the pain intensified. Nothing was going to stop her. She told herself stubbornly. But where could he be? She looked up worriedly, at the sky. The sun had almost gone. It will all be dark soon. Thirty minutes into her search and she began to realize how ridiculous it was. If the villagers who had known him, longer than she, could not find him, how was she to? Maybe, he'd find me. He would give me some sign when he gets a glimpse of me. She looked at her ankle and noticed it had swollen slightly. She laughed.

"I know your tricks!" She shouted into the air. "Is that all you've got? You think this can stop me?" Suddenly, the sun disappeared beyond the horizon, leaving a total blackout. She whipped out her phone and checked the time displaying on the screen. It was 5mins past 7.
"This is normal." She muttered to herself, as she put on the phone's touch. "Nothing to be scared of." An owl hooted from a tree nearby. Juanita quickened her step.

"Though I walk through the valley of the shadow of death…"

"I will forgive you if you take my hand and join me." Her mother, in a wrapper, walked beside her.

"…I will fear no evil."

"Don't be stubborn! You ignorant child." Her mother still hurried after her. "I'm really not dead, I just live in the other world beyond. Come!" She touched her arm, and Juanita screamed,

"Jesus!" and shut her eyes. When she opened it, she was alone again. She started running as fast as her hurting leg would let her.

"Ok, God. I am not much of a prayer warrior, but I really need your help."

"You are beyond help!"

Juanita stopped on her tracks. The moon came out and its light revealed the beautiful Igugu Igbe priestess, standing a few feet in front, blocking her path. She stood with her legs apart and her hands planted on her waist. Dressed in a white wrapper and red scarf tied around her waist, she looked ready for battle.
"A bird that flies from the ground unto an Anthill, does not know that it is still on the ground."

Juanita massaged her temple. "And who might you be?"

"I am the great priestess of Igugu, the one and only true Igbe god, Mother of all."

"Wow, so many responsibilities on your tiny self." She eyed the lady who looked like her age mate. She could probably fight a physical battle with her and win.

"The size of a drum is not determined by its size, nor the skills of a drummer, but by his strength. Your grandma was fooled by my size too." The priestess laughed. "But she soon found out the truth."

"Well, you can't blame her. I mean, seeing my mother's apparition scares me, but you...you wouldn't even sell in a Nollywood witch scene."

"Enough!" Her voice rumbled like thunder and the bushes shook furiously. Juanita shivered in fear, she had angered the witch. But she was so tired of the nonsense. She couldn't care less, what she could do to her.

"It's nice chatting with you and all, but if you don't mind, I got a friend to look for."

"Oh, I mind. I mind a lot. And your so-called friend, that idiot who could not mind his business, and is trying to spoil what has been for decades, shall die tonight. He will be cut in bits, and his carcass set ablaze. And guess what?" Juanita didn't have the nerve to guess.
"I will have no hand in it. It will all be the villagers doing. They will catch him just at the outskirt of the village, trying to escape. How fun is that?" She shrieked out what was supposed to be laughter, causing Juanita to wince. "Who's going to save you now, pretty girl?"

"Well," Juanita tried to look nonchalant, without success. "...that same God is not dead. He's here with me." An uncanny silence swept over them for a few seconds.

"You are a fool." She began to pace. As if planning how to trap her prey. "You do not know that your God respects covenant and you've been pledged to us. What is done, can never be undone!" She stamped her feet, hard. The ground shook and Juanita fell, but she stood up quickly.

"But it has." She replied defiantly. "I renounced you. I don't belong to you anymore!"

"You cannot!" She stamped her foot again, and this time, Juanita saw from a distance, two ladies clad in white coming from behind her. She could have sworn she heard the rhythmic beat of talking drums. She closed her eyes and saw the river. She opened it quickly. Her ankle began to hurt so bad, she fell to the ground, screaming in pain. Her eyes closed and she saw her mother weeping profusely, by the river. She quickly opened it again, and the priestess was standing before her, snarling.

"Lord, please don't abandon me now," Juanita muttered under her breath.
"You cannot renounce what the strong blood of a maiden had spoken." She grabbed her by the

neck, strangling her. She let her go, laughing and enjoying the torture, even as Juanita coughed and gasped for breath.

"You can touch me. You can hold me." Juanita managed to say in disbelief.

She frowned. "Of course, I can." She laughed. "I can imagine your small mind thinking I was a spirit."

"Oh, that's good. So I can do this…" With one swift move, she brought out the kitchen knife, from her pocket, and slashed the witch's throat. She dodged the falling body and scrambled to her feet, hopping, running and stumbling, even as she looked back to see the two women run to meet their dying priestess. Juanita ran into the night, headed for the outskirts of town, with only one thing in mind… saving Tega. She didn't see the shaky hand of the priestess, take the knife and slice the neck of one of her followers, while the other watched in fear, as she sucked the blood of the maiden, declaring words in an unknown tongue. Lightning struck, thunder rumbled, the trees swayed angrily. With blood flowing from her mouth and wound no longer bleeding, the priestess howled into the night.

Juanita heard the sickening howl of an animal and she continued to run. She had to get to Tega. She had to help him somehow. She couldn't let him die. The night was cool, still, she sweated. Her movement slowed down, she was dragging her leg by now. Tears poured down her eyes as her right leg got heavy. She collapsed against a tree trunk and wept. This was not the life she bargained for. Never in her wildest dream, would she have imagined herself far away from home in a barbaric backward town. She should have been pursuing her dreams, making partner at the firm, planning her wedding with Craig. That idiot. Who could blame him? Could he handle what Tega was going through now because of her? She dozed off.
A big mosquito sang by her ear, when she didn't budge, it bit her on the cheek. She slapped her left cheek as she jolted up. Then she checked the time on her phone and couldn't believe it was 5:00 am.

"Tega!" She jumped up, tested her ankle which was surprisingly better and began to run. She had slept for hours, she hoped she wasn't too late.

She heard their voices before she saw them. A crowd yelling and pushing each other, to get a better view, with the late risers, especially the elderlies, just joining in, to catch a piece of the action. Juanita feared what must have happened. She knew Tega had been caught from the shouts all around. Don't these people sleep? She guessed in a town like this one, this must be one of their biggest entertainment.

"Kill am, burn am!" The people chanted. She could hear the sound of wood hitting flesh. Then she heard a bottle break. She saw a policeman laughing at the event and rushed to meet him.

"Sir, do something. They will kill him."

He scowled at her. "Do what? This na jungle justice na."

"Aren't you supposed to protect and bring law and order?"

"Woman, it will be my life on the line here, if I try anything. Those guys are in charge here." He pointed to a tall guy in front, with a pistol hung loosely on his shoulder. She still couldn't see Tega, as most of the people in front were taller, so she ran to an orange tree, by the side, where three boys of about 12 were hanging from. She tried to climb the tree, but kept slipping back. The boys exchanged glances, then burst out laughing.

"Why don't you help me up, instead of laughing?" She spat out. The boys looked at themselves again, then one of them stretched out his palm, but when she tried to take it, he withdrew it and frowned at her blank look. Then he stretched it out again, and understanding dawned on her. She dipped her hand into her pocket and brought out N1000, the boy frowned. Are these kids? She wondered as she added N500, he grabbed it, and pocketed it, with the other two staring hungrily at the pocket. Then, the three of them grabbed her hands, hoisted her up and let her sit on a branch. She saw him immediately. He was bleeding from the head and body. He was shirtless. One guy picked a block and threw it on him, causing it to break on him. Tears blinded Juanita's eyes. She wiped her face with her palm, as she watched with dread, another youth, poured fuel on two big tyres, dragged it and placed it on top Tega. The crowd got excited. They were going to burn him. Tega tried to push off the tyres, but Apko struck him with a big stick. Fear and rage combined, Juanita scrambled down the tree, shoved and pushed until she got to the front, then she grabbed the gun from the tall man's shoulder and aimed at the crowd.

"Step back!" She shouted at the tyre boy and Apko, who obeyed immediately, joining the crowd to stare dazed at her. Tega raised his swollen eyes at her, and she saw hope. She raised her voice. "Anybody move, and I'll shoot!"

The tall man chuckled and spat tobacco out of his mouth. "You sabi shoot sef? Shey my hunting gun resemble toy for your eye?"

She looked at Tega again, his eyes seemed to be asking her the same question. She could tell he knew the answer, because, he began to remove the tyres.
"Play cool." He croaked.

"You will find out if you move!" She shouted back at the crowd. He moved. Shit. It was a step, to test her. "I'm warning you!" Another step. Tega removed the second tyre, and struggled to his feet, coughing out blood. He held on to Juanita and they began to step back.
"Stay back!"

The crowd began to laugh, some were still confused, though.

"This one no sabi o." Oke said.

A village drunk laughed, with his bottle tucked under his armpit. "This American Wonder, does not knoweth that she will pull that cock back, aim and fire. What a waste of brain, I tell you. I, The Professor, tell you."

Obruche slapped his head from behind. "Shut up! Mad Prof."

"Collect the gun jor!" Apko angrily moved towards Juanita, but she did as the drunkard had said and fired. Apko grabbed the barrel of the pistol, as he went down, she grabbed it from his hand and shot into the air. The crowd stepped back, watching Apko bleed from the stomach, in disbelief. Oh God, what had she done? Now, she was a fugitive.

"Let's go!" Tega jolted her. They began to run out of town.

"Naso dem go escape?" One woman, dressed like a man on khaki, big shirt and red bandana tied on her forehead, asked. "We no fit let them go na!"
The tall hunter watched Apko, breathe his last and give up the ghost. Rage surged through him and he began to chase after them, the Khaki woman joined, the villagers cried out and joined the chase, stepping on Apko's corpse as they ran.

Juanita dreaded killing another person, but she shot at the hunter and missed. The bullet hit the Khaki woman on the left leg and she tumbled on the ground, howling in pain.
"Kill that Oyinbo witch!" She exclaimed. Juanita tried to shoot again, but it was empty. Not now! She panicked.

"Run, Ani!" Tega, with all his strength, dragged her along. They had an advantage of a little distance, but they knew it wasn't going to be for long, as the hunter was gaining in on them. They needed a miracle. Tega was injured. Juanita was tired. There was no hope. They were out of town, nowhere to hide. Just dry large expanse of road. They were going to die. That realization hit her like a bullet, in her chest. She held Tega tighter, causing him to glance at her. She could see the fear in his eyes. She smiled sadly.

"I'm sorry." She managed to breathe out, as they were still running. "You should have left me like Craig did. You don't deserve this."

"What nonsense are you saying?" He shouted. "I love you. You die, I die, remember?"

Tears welled up in her eyes, blinding her, but she still ran. "I love you too. I'm sorry we don't have much time. You'd have been the best Boo, ever."

Tega laughed in spite of himself. "Boo? I kind of prefer, husband."

Juanita laughed and cried. "I wish I could give you that too."

Tega's eyes narrowed. "You're serious?" She nodded. "You really love me?" She nodded again. "Then we can't die. Not now. Not here." He looked up. "God, we want to live, we need a miracle."

Juanita smiled sadly at his faith, but she knew they were doomed. The crowd was cheering because they were so close. The hunter was actually grinning.

The sun began to rise and Juanita saw it. Tega had seen it too, because he tightened his grip, and picked up speed. Was this the miracle? A bike sitting by the road all by itself. Was the key in the ignition? Yes, it was! Juanita confirmed joyfully as Tega jumped on it. He started the engine as she got behind him.

"Ojhi! Ojhi o!" Shouting thief, in Urhobo, a man ran out of a little bush by the roadside, with his trouser still down. Tega reversed the bike, even as the hunter got to them, swinging a punch at Tega, who ducked and zoomed off. The crowd began throwing stones, but the bike was already too far. They just watched it kick dust, as it sped away.

*　　*　　*　　*　　*

Tega's sister ran out of the kitchen with a bowl of hot water and a towel. She went into a bedroom, where Juanita was hunched over Tega, who was sprawled on the bed.

"I insist you go to the hospital. This is too much. I'm not a nurse!" Eno cried out.

Juanita held his hand. "Listen to your sister, Tega. We are out of danger now. The villagers can't find us here. You said they won't come all that way. This is Warri."

"It's not the villagers I'm worried about." Tega moaned. "It's the Igbe." His head had stopped bleeding, but there was a big gash by the side, and it caused a massive headache. His body was filled with bloodlines from the stick he had been beaten with.

"But the priestess is dead," Juanita said, as she gave way for Eno to tend to her brother's wounds.

"Did you see her die?"

"Well, no."

"Then I'm not letting you out of my sight."

"You're no use to me dead." She argued.

"Just shut up, Juanita." He groaned as Eno pressed his body.

"This is just foolish." Eno shook her head in disapproval. "You have lost so much, all for what? I didn't go to work because of this. Let my husband return, and talk some sense into you, on how not to get involved with a daughter of Igbe." She spat out.

"Eno, please…" Tega began.

"Your life, your decision." She cut in. "But I won't sit while you throw everything away."

Juanita sighed. "For what it's worth, I'm truly sorry. I told him to back off, but he wouldn't. Plus, I can assure you, he's out of danger now."

Eno laughed and looked her over. "Under normal circumstance, I'd gladly welcome you, knowing my brother crushed on you for years, we teased him about it. But surely, you don't expect me to hug you, seeing you're the reason the only house we have in the village is gone and he nearly lost his life."

Juanita bowed her head. "I understand."

"Good. Now, make yourself useful and fetch me the first aid box, from the storeroom, go through the kitchen."

"Yes ma. " She eagerly rushed out of the room.

Tega rolled his eyes at his sister. "Tyrant."

"Somebody has to be." She snorted.

It was 11:30 pm. Eno's husband had returned and was still talking to Tega.
Didn't they realize he should be resting? Juanita wondered, as she dozed on and off on the cream long cushion in the living room. Her eyes closed again and she saw the priestess face, smirking at her. She bolted upright. This wasn't over yet. And Tega was in a bad shape. Could she come here? Could that demon know where they were? Then she heard Tega suddenly let out an agonizing cry. She rushed to the room and found husband and wife hunched over him, trying to hold him down. Tega, on the other hand, was holding his head.

"It hurts! It hurts! Make it stop!"

"Get the car." Eno snapped at her husband. He hurried out of the room. "Easy, kid brother, we're going to the hospital. What is taking you so long?" She shouted at her already departed husband. Her gaze settled on Juanita who looked like she was about to cry. "Be strong, woman, he doesn't need your tears now." Juanita nodded and helped in holding Tega down. She began to hum an unknown lullaby and Eno frowned. She was about to ask her what she was doing but she noticed Tega wasn't writhing anymore. Juanita climbed the bed and placed his head on her lap, humming and patting him softly. He seemed totally at peace, but the silence was broken when Eno's husband rushed back in.

"The car won't start." He was panting.

Eno frowned. "What do you mean, but you drove it back from work?"

"Babe, I'm not a mechanic. I don't know what happened." He was on edge too. He looked at Tega. "He seems fine now."

Eno's eyes narrowed. "We are still going to the hospital. He's my only brother!"

"You want us to go out by a few minutes to midnight? In Warri town? Do you want to get us lynched?"

"I will lynch you if my brother dies! How about that?" He looked at her fiery eyes and swallowed. He knew the woman he had married. He went to their side and began to help lift him up.
"Two of you should get him outside, I'm calling a friend to pick us up." Eno dictated as she hurried out to get her phone. She met them outside, staring at the sky, even as the clock struck twelve.

"What is it?" Lightning struck a cable wire, causing it to spark aggressively as it cut and hit the ground. They jumped back. Eno screwed her face. "Let's go!"
Thunder followed, shaking the ground.

"It's going to rain!" Her husband shouted.

"Let's keep going!" Juanita shouted back, and looked at Eno, who nodded in agreement. They only took a step. The rain came down, like it was letting the whole of heaven loose. Big fat raindrops slapped and forced them back into the house.

"The elements are sure against us tonight." The husband slammed the door behind them shaking water from his already drenched white shirt.

"Not the elements." Eno's eyes met Juanita's knowingly. Tega screamed, falling to the floor and holding his head.

"Not again!" Eno crouched, holding him. "Get me ice and towel." She told her husband. He came back with it. Eno after a while would send him off on another errand, nothing was working, Juanita realized.

"Don't let me die!" Tega screamed. "Stop- the drum! Stop the drum!"

"He's hallucinating." Her husband said, fearfully.

"They are beating his head like a drum! It's them! It's Igbe!" She looked at Juanita. "He's been telling me to be serious, spiritually. I'm not a prayer warrior, so if he taught you anything, now is the time!" But Juanita couldn't say anything, she just watched Tega, dying. Then she heard it. The drum. It sounded like the thunder outside was playing a pestle and mortar game. She looked at the door, then, at them, praying on the floor. Eno raised her head up and looked at her.
Eno shook her head. "Don't do it." Tears flooded Juanita's eyes. "This is not what Tega wants." But Juanita backed up against the door. "Are you listening to me? Get back here at once!" Eno jumped up, but Juanita was faster. She grabbed the key, from the keyhole, opened the door and stepped outside, slammed the door and locked them in, just as Eno got to it, hitting it repeatedly and demanding she opened it.

"Arrrrrgh!" Eno screamed and kicked the door. "Stupid brat!"

"Calm down. This is her fight, not yours." Her husband called, from where he was still holding Tega.

"But she will get herself killed. What do I tell Tega when he gets better?" Her eyes lit up. "The back door!" She sprang for the kitchen, but her husband grabbed her arms, abandoning Tega.

"Well, there will be no telling, if he dies now. Would there? Use your head, Babe. I'm not losing you too. She did the right thing."

She shook his grip off. "She's dead already. And it's on you to explain to Tega." She knelt beside her brother, murmuring prayers, while he stood, looking frustrated.

Juanita entered the rain. She knew she was out there, somewhere.

"Come out bitch, and let's finish this once and for all!" She yelled into the storm. The trees around shook mightily, snapping branches and swinging wood up to five feet. The roof of a kiosk nearby came off, and swung towards Juanita, she ducked and it crashed against the window, shattering the glass.
Juanita laughed. "You know what you remind me of? A dog with a big bark, but no teeth!" She screamed as a sharp object sliced through her back. She turned and saw the knife clatter to the ground. It was her Nana's kitchen knife. She picked it, with her blood dripping from it.

"Coward! Face me!" She stepped back as the priestess suddenly materialized before her. With the knife firmly in her grasp, she thrust it into the witch's chest. "Die bitch!"
But the knife didn't go through. The priestess laughed wickedly, picked her up by the shoulders, and threw her against the door. Juanita moaned in pain.

"I underestimated you the first time" growled the Priestess. "Fool me twice, then I'm not the daughter of the great Igugu. Even if you fired a bazooka, it will not penetrate for I have fortified myself. In this business, sister, you are a learner!"

Juanita frowned. "Wait, I am your sister."

The priestess stared blankly at her. "It was a figure of speech, stupid. Are you not the one from the English world?"

"No, no, no. Not that." She stood up, with some effort. "I mean, if I'm truly a daughter of Igugu Igbe like you, then we are sisters. Why do you want to kill your sister?"

The priestess smiled sweetly. "Nice try. But you weren't meant to live long. Serve, then die and return to where you came from. And if my grandma could kill my mother for defying the true god, how much more you, a common nobody?"

"But I'm not a reincarnate. Where am I returning to? Have you died before? Do you know the spirit life?"

The priestess looked confused. "Silence!" She shouted. Then she chuckled. "You're trying to get to me, but you do not have any inkling as to how much I hate you. I had to return to the village after my mother died. I was tortured too. I had to serve! I left school! Left my fiancé! Left everything I knew and owned in Lagos, to come serve. And you, the Yankee babe, you want to go scout free? Never! After what you did?"

"What did I do?" Juanita threw her hands up in exasperation.

"You and your stupid new lover! Stuffing his nose in matters that do not concern him. At least, your foreign idiot was wise enough to tuck his tail between his legs and run, as I told him to. But not Tega, he proved to be stronger than most pastors. While you people prayed, my mirrors broke, and instantly, two of my maidens died. My shrine has collapsed. And yet you won't stop. Do you know I had to kill another of my maiden because you slit my throat? I took her life, in exchange for mine. The others have all ran away. I will get them and teach them all a lesson! You, I will enjoy killing. No Tega to help you now, no weapon either." She laughed hysterically, as she approached Juanita.

"Aren't you forgetting something?" Juanita asked defiantly.

"What?"

"Jesus."

The priestess screwed her face until it was hideous, she raised her hands, and the wind rose with her. "If mere men could be called rainmakers, I am the Storm." She moved her hands swiftly towards Juanita, who upon seeing what was happening, began to run, but the wind picked her up and threw her into a tree, her body slammed it, and she slumped to the floor. "I would like to see Jesus save you now!"

"Don't sound so smug." Juanita coughed out blood. "I will win this. I'm a lawyer you know. Plus Tega said all I have to do is renounce you and I'm free."

The witch ran to her and slapped her twice, dragging her by the hair, while Juanita struggled to free herself. "Do you look free? Hmm? Tell me! I will teach you to fear me!" She grabbed her by the neck and lifted her off the ground. While Juanita dangled, she noticed the deep gash on the witch's neck, where she had cut her. She stretched her hand and snapped a twig from the tree. "I told you before, no sacrifice is greater than the blood of a maiden. You cannot renounce us!" Juanita jabbed the twig into the wound and the priestess dropped her but stepped on her injured ankle before she could run.

"Oh yes I can!" Juanita winced in pain. "By the blood of Jesus, which is higher than any other blood, I renounce you, and I break your fortitude!" She screamed in pain, as she forcefully dragged her ankle from the priestess grip, rose up and forced the twig into the wound. This time it went through. The witch screamed and her blood splattered on Juanita's face. She picked her and threw her up. Juanita landed on her back with a loud thud and yelped as the witch pounced on her, ready to bite her neck, showing teeth, like fangs. Juanita pulled out the twig from her attacker's neck and pierced her eyes. The priestess fell back, howling in pain and holding her right eyes. Juanita stumbled to her feet, searching for the knife. The priestess crawled towards her, moaning like a wounded animal.

She placed her hand on the ground. "From the- water you came…" She said with effort, "…to the water shall you return. Igugu ooooo!" She slapped the wet ground, and a flood began to take shape. Water pooled all around them, as the rain poured heavier. Juanita dipped her hands into the water blindly and searched frantically for the knife. I can't die like this, she thought. I was winning already! She watched as the priestess began to twirl a finger. The waters rose and began a violent rotating windstorm, forming a cyclone and rapidly growing. The water picked Juanita up and she fell back into it. She managed to gain her feet and raised her head for air.

"He that the lord set free, is free indeed." Juanita sucked in air, just as the waters covered them both. She went down on all fours and scrambled about in the sand, her hand finally gripped the knife, just as the priestess reached her. She stabbed her repeatedly on the already bleeding wound. "I am not a child of Igbe! I do not come from the water! I am a child of the living God! Die, motherfucker!" She stabbed her one last time in the right eye. The priestess let out a heart rendering shriek and the waters got violent, picking them up. They were going to be carried away by the cyclone. They began to twirl with the water and Juanita screamed, but a firm hand grabbed her. It was Tega. A rope was tied around his waist and he began to move back gingerly, but the current was strong, trying to keep them in the swirling funnel. He held her to himself, and Juanita circled her hands around him. She began to pray and noticed they were moving backwards. They came out of the cyclone, with Eno and her husband pulling at the rope, with all their strength. They all tumbled to the ground and watched as the cyclone moved rapidly away and disappeared with the priestess animalistic cry, feeling the air. The rain began to drizzle and finally stopped. They looked at each other and Tega smiled weakly at Juanita.

"It's finally over."

EPILOGUE

Tega climbed the staircase and went into the veranda, where Juanita was standing by the bannister. She looked like a beautiful angel, wearing a white dress shirt, slightly above her knee. The soft breeze tossed her long dark braids round her face, even as she stared at a portrait. She raised her head and smiled at him. His heart melted and he stood still for a few seconds before he walked up to her, and held her from behind. He looked at the picture of her mum. She was an older version of Juanita. Dressed in a blue lace attire and gold George, she smiled at the camera, her eyes crinkling with laughter.

"You're breathtaking." He whispered into her ear.

She giggled. "Me or my mum?"

"You." He planted a kiss on her neck and Juanita turned her face towards him.

"Stop kidding around. How was your trip?" They were in Lagos City, at her mother's duplex. It's been a month since the whole incident. Tega had gone to the village to settle the rape matter, even though she had vehemently refused. "It must have gone well since you are in a good mood. Did the elders believe you?"

"Oh, I didn't have to convince them. The perpetrators were none other than Obruche and Apko. Obruche was caught, trying to rape Oke, in the bush. After much beating from the youths, he confessed they raped Ikebe, but then she died, which wasn't their plan. They figured they could blame it on me since her corpse was in my house.

"And Apko?" She clenched her right fist.

He unclenched it and linked his fingers through hers. "He's dead. And don't beat yourself about it. You didn't mean to kill him. Besides, the villagers think he deserved it. He's been a really bad boy. After the incident with Ikebe, girls have been coming out to say how they've been raped and threatened to be killed if they spoke up. Obruche was burnt alive.

"Jeez."

Tega shrugged. "The same fate would have met Apko. You seemed to have eased his death."

"This is not right. The villagers can't keep taking laws into their own hands, deciding who should live and who shouldn't.

He sighed. "It's called jungle justice. Especially when there is no trust in our security system. Enough of that. Did you see your father?"

Juanita looked at the portrait. "Not now. Maybe sometime in the future."

"Speaking of future? Will you still spend it with me? Will you stay here in Lagos?" Tega held his breath.

Juanita looked at the beautiful blue sky, then massaged her temple. "I'm going to America…" Tega bowed his head in disappointment. "…to resign properly and get my properties in order. Then, I'll return here to live in my mum's house…and see about that future with you."
Tega's head flew up, and she laughed at his comic expression. He laughed too, and picked her up, twirling her around. They were going to be okay, Juanita thought; even as she closed her eyes and let the cool breeze caress her face.

THE END.